He Wanted Her. His Love Might Be Dead—He Said It Was, And She Believed Him— But Salah Wanted Her.

Closure. That was such an extraordinary thing for a man like Salah to say! What closure would sex give him? *You have haunted me, Desi.* Was it true? Or did he have some ulterior motive for saying it?

The intimacy of the roof garden. The constant harking on the past. The fact he had ordered food he had lovingly described to her ten years ago. The irresistible way he'd chosen tidbits for her, fed her. Painful reminders of their love, scorching tokens of intimacy, the actions of a man determined to win back an old love.

All false. All stage dressing. Salah did not want to win her back. He had made that very plain, a long time ago.

Why, then?

He wants revenge. The thought dropped into her head with an almost audible click. Four days. Five. He could find a dozen ways to get revenge, she was sure, alone with her in the desert for five days. But what did he want revenge *for?*

Dear Reader,

I wonder how many men and women hold in their hearts the image of their first love while they carry on lives that bear no relation to that dream? For every story that we hear of true love reunited—after years, even decades of separation—there must be many, many more who remember, but never take that risky first step toward rediscovery. If the chance was offered, though, would we be able to resist?

My heroine, Desi, hasn't kept the dream alive, at least not consciously. A painful betrayal changed her passionate young love, first to its opposite, and then to indifference—or so she imagines. It would take wild horses for her to seek out her old love, Salah…wild horses, or a best friend's desperate need.

Salah, now a powerful Cup Companion who has the confidence of a prince, also thinks himself immune to the siren call of rediscovered love. But still he is driven to meet Desi, the first love whose memory has haunted him all these years. And once met, he's driven to taste the bittersweetness again.…

There's another kind of reunion for me in this book—it's my first SONS OF THE DESERT story in nearly five years. I'm very glad to be back writing for you again, and I hope you'll find the rediscovery as thrilling as I do!

Love,

Alexandra Sellers

ALEXANDRA SELLERS

SHEIKH'S BETRAYAL

Silhouette®

Desire

Published by Silhouette Books

America's Publisher of Contemporary Romance

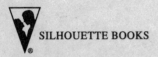

SILHOUETTE BOOKS

ISBN-13: 978-0-373-76959-9

SHEIKH'S BETRAYAL

Recycling programs
for this product may
not exist in your area.

Visit Silhouette Books at www.eHarlequin.com

Printed in U.S.A.

Books by Alexandra Sellers

Silhouette Desire

Sheikh's Ransom #1210
The Solitary Sheikh #1217
Beloved Sheikh #1221
Occupation: Casanova #1264
Sheikh's Temptation #1274
Sheikh's Honor #1294
Sheikh's Woman #1341
The Sultan's Heir #1379
Undercover Sultan #1385
Sleeping with the Sultan #1391
The Playboy Sheikh #1417
Sheikh's Castaway #1618
The Ice Maiden's Sheikh #1623
The Fierce and Tender Sheikh #1629
Sheikh's Betrayal #1959

*Sons of the Desert

ALEXANDRA SELLERS

is an author of more than twenty-five novels and a feline language text published in 1997 and still selling.

Born and raised in Canada, Alexandra first moved to London as a drama student. Now she lives near Hampstead Heath with her husband, Nick. They share housekeeping with Monsieur, who jumped through the window one day and announced, as cats do, that he was moving in.

What she would miss most on a desert island is shared laughter.

Readers can write to Alexandra at P.O. Box 9449, London NW3 2WH, England.

For you,

Again

Prologue

There were two immigration officers at passport control, and a short line of travellers in front of each. A man stood behind one of the desks, scanning the faces of the disembarking passengers. His watchful stillness was a hub for the busy flow, as if the scene somehow revolved around him.

He looked straight at Desi, and a buzz of warning sounded in her bones. She was wearing sunglasses, but even so, she turned her head to avoid meeting his eyes. Passport and landing card in her hand, clutching her elegantly travel-worn leather bag, she joined the other line, and resolutely did not look his way again.

But it had taken only one glance for his image to get stuck in her memory, as irritating as a fishbone: desert dark and harsh-faced, wearing an immaculate white cotton kaftan under a flowing burnous and the traditional headscarf she knew was called a *keffiyeh*. A chiselled mouth. Cheeks carved out of the rock she'd flown over in the desert, a scar across one cheekbone.

"Passport, please," a voice said, and Desi came to. It was her turn. She stepped forward and handed up her passport. She was tight with nerves.

Desirée Drummond. He read the name without a flicker of recognition, and she breathed a little easier.

"Take off sunglasses, please."

She had to comply. She held her breath while the agent's eyes roved over her face with sudden eagerness. She let it out slowly when it was clear he didn't recognize her face, either. He didn't ask her to take off her hat. He picked up his official stamp and flipped through the heavily stamped passport for an empty page.

"What is porpoise of visit?"

"Pleasure." *And that's the first lie done and dusted,* she told herself. *Pleasure is the last thing I expect from this little outing.* Then, an inexpert liar, she rushed to add detail. "I'm a student of archaeology. I'm going to visit a dig."

"Deeg?" he was clearly pleased to have an excuse to prolong the encounter. He might not have recognized her, but he clearly liked what he saw. "What is *deeg?*"

"Oh…it's a—a place where they find an ancient city or something and…archaeologists, you know, they dig to find out about history."

His eyes widened with sudden alertness, and Desi cursed herself. Why hadn't she just left well enough alone?

"Where is the dig?" he asked, in the voice of a man determined not to let beauty distract him from duty.

"Oh!" Desi laughed awkwardly. "I don't actually know. Someone is meeting me…."

"Stamp the passport," a deep voice commanded in Arabic, and both heads snapped up in surprise.

Him. The man who had been watching her. Standing by the immigration officer now and looking at Desi with a black gaze that sent nervous ripples down her spine.

Then she gasped, her head snapping back in sudden shock. The face of the stranger in front of her dissolved and reassembled. Her heart kicked like a million volts.

"I don't believe it!" she croaked.

"Hello, Desi," he said, in the same second.

"Salah?"

He was nothing like the boy she remembered, nor the man she might have imagined that boy becoming. He looked closer to forty than thirty. There were deep lines on his forehead, a scar high on one cheek, and the once-generous mouth was tight and disciplined. The thin boy's chest and shoulders had filled out with mature muscle.

And those were only the superficial changes. He had an aura of unquestioned authority, a man used to commanding and being obeyed. Power came off him like heat, distorting the air around him.

But it was the harshness, the cold disillusion behind the eyes that shocked her most.

Salah, but not Salah. She could not imagine how he'd got here from who he had been. She was looking at a stranger.

A stranger whose name, she knew, was His Excellency Salahuddin Nadim ibn Khaled ibn Shukri al Khouri, Cup Companion to Prince Omar of the Barakat Emirates, one of the dozen most influential men in his government.

The childhood sweetheart she had come here to seduce, and betray.

One

"Baba's a gineer."

That mystical communication, imparted to Desirée by Samiha on their first day at school, had entranced Desi with its exotic otherness and bound her instantly to her pretty, dark-eyed new friend. Soon she learned that *Baba* meant *Daddy,* and that *gineer* meant he had come to the west coast to build something big. But the magic never quite faded.

It was the first day of what grew into a lifelong friendship. Desi and Sami were inseparable all through school. They spent their summers together, too, on a small island off the B.C. coast, where the Drummond family's lakefront "cottage" was a century-old black clapboard farmhouse with outbuildings.

Her ex-hippie parents were hoping to turn the place into a year-round home, growing their own food, and hosting retreats, healing courses, and dream workshops in the summer to see them through the winter. But the project never generated enough income for her father to give up his university post and permanently move the family from Vancouver.

Every summer Desi and her brother and sister were each allowed to invite a friend to stay. Every year from first grade on, Desi took Sami.

The summer Desi turned nine, Samiha's cousin Salah came from Central Barakat to stay with Sami's family and improve his English. Salah was twelve, the same age as her brother Harry, and for some reason no one could afterwards remember, he was invited to the cottage.

Salah and Harry became friends, and after that every year it was somehow taken for granted that Salah would be a part of their summer adventure.

Salah was deeply attractive, a fascinating boy. Those first few summers, Desi hovered between hero worship and competitiveness in her feelings for him, half determined to prove she was braver and brighter than any boy, half wishing Salah were *her* friend instead of her brother's.

Such feelings were a perfect primer for something deeper, and it wasn't long in coming. At the end of the summer she turned fourteen, Desi was just entering on puberty, and a new awareness between herself and Salah beckoned. The next summer, Salah didn't make his annual visit to Canada.

During those two years, Desi grew up. Her breasts formed, her waist appeared, and her height shot up six inches that was almost all leg. Her face shifted from sweet roundness to a haunting elegance.

The just-sixteen-year-old who greeted her old sparring partner the following summer was tall, very slender, and quirkily beautiful—so "unusual" that she had been spotted in the street by a scout and signed with a modelling agency.

As for Salah, at nineteen he showed more clearly the man he would be: slim but powerful, with broad, thin shoulders, a dark, intense gaze and a voice that came from his toes. He was also broody, inscrutable, and very sure of his opinions.

Of course she fell in love with him. Of course she did. The friend of childhood whom she already adored, transformed into a romantic hero? Salah was now intensely good-looking, darkly masculine—and so much more adult than the boys at school. And his innocent integrity was a complete contrast to the predatory male sleaze her father and minders kept at a distance in the modelling world.

He was clearly sunk by the new Desi, whose flowing hair moved even when she didn't, whose creamy skin glowed with sensual promise, whose bikinis showed off the curve of full small breasts, fabulous legs, smooth abdomen, and firm rump, and who could scarcely eat for fear of gaining an ounce.

That was the year, by an unlucky coincidence—though they thought it perfect enough then—that both her brother Harry and her friend Sami missed the usual holiday on the island. Samiha had gone back to the Barakat Emirates for a visit, and at the last minute Harry had got a summer job to earn money for university. He came to the island only on odd weekends.

It was only natural that Desi and Salah should spend their time with each other.

That summer, too, there was a heat wave, and maybe it was the exhaustion factor that meant her parents didn't notice the building chemical reaction between them, or maybe it was just their hippy laissez-faire attitude; Desi never knew.

On the mainland there were forest fires, but the islands, although oven-hot during the day, mercifully got rain at night. Mornings began cool and fresh, with mist lifting off the lake, but by ten the temperature was soaring, and by eleven most of the paying guests were prostrated by the heat.

Everybody hated the intense heat—everybody except Desi

and Salah. Salah was used to such temperatures, and as for Desi—she felt she was waking from a lifelong sleep. The heat energized her, made her blood sing, her muscles flex, as if she were a runner waiting to begin a race she knew she'd win.

Not just the heat, of course, contributed to the feeling.

They became inseparable. Looking back on that summer, Desi remembered bright hot days lasting forever, and an all-encompassing joy in sheer being. They ran together, swam together, talked, explored.

They didn't stop competing with each other, of course. But that only added to the intensity, spiced their meetings, kept them on their toes.

"Salah?"

They gazed at each other for a frozen moment, and suddenly, treacherously, against all the odds, the warm, sweet, sensual memories of a decade ago stirred to melting in her. The sun-burnt warmth of his naked chest against her trembling hand. Black eyes filled with love and need. The intoxication of desire that he had tried so nobly to resist....

Kiss him hello. You need to knock him off balance right at the start, before he gets his lines of control in place.

Desi couldn't have moved to save her life. She couldn't have kissed Salah to save the world. All she could do was stand there, her gaze locked with his, and wonder how she would ever manage to do what she had come here to do, while yesterday's vision of a full, young, passionate mouth and eyes intense with longing arose to confuse the impression of tight control and harsh judgement she saw in his face now.

Then his mouth moved.

"Who were you expecting?"

"Not you."

If he had expected anything, it was not that his heart would leap so painfully at his first glimpse of her. This fact annoyed him almost as much as her daring to come here. It argued a weakness in him, and he would not be weak where she was concerned. He was no longer a boy, to be at the mercy of his own needs, and hers. He would not be manipulated by her sexuality, practised as it was. He was a man, as she would discover.

Her right eyebrow flared up in the nervous way he remembered. Her eyes seemed slate grey now, as if her anxiety had drained them of colour. She had chameleon eyes, a fact he remembered well. He had never met a woman whose eyes changed colour in such a way. In his memory they were mostly turquoise, deep and rich, like the jewel. Green sometimes when they made love in daylight…and sometimes this green-tinged, slate grey….

"I was not expecting you, either," he said grimly.

"Then I wonder who you're here to meet."

"I hoped that you would change your mind. You should have."

"Excellency," the passport officer murmured, and His Excellency Salahuddin Nadim al Khouri surfaced to take her passport from the outstretched hand. A muscle in his jaw moved.

"Come, Desi," he said, turning to lead the way. He pronounced it, as he always had, *Deezee*. The memories it summoned up skated on her nerves. *Desi, I love you. I will love you longer than the stars burn.*

Now that the gaze was broken, she could move. She fell into step beside but a little behind him. *Like a good Muslim wife,* she told herself, and with an irritated little skip that was totally unlike her, she caught up with him.

Her heart was in turmoil, not least because of the way he had changed. Was this what the desert did? Was this the kind of man it grew? Fierce, hard…dangerous to cross?

But she had to cross him. She had come here to cross him.

I'm sure he never got over you. He'd probably give his right arm for the chance to kiss you.

She had even believed that she would enjoy settling scores with him. What a fool she was. If anyone was going to suffer from their encounter, it would not be this closed, proud man.

He led her through a door marked with an elegant sweep of Arabic letters above *Private* in English. They passed along an empty corridor in charged silence. She tried to think of something ordinary to say. If only he would ask her about the flight! Couldn't he feel how the silence built tension? Or didn't he care?

"We flew in over the Barakati desert," she offered, stupidly, because how else would a plane get to the capital of Central Barakat? "It's the first time I've seen desert like that! It's so…well, *beautiful* is the wrong word. It has a haunting…"

He turned his head and her little speech died as the black gaze collided with her own.

"People have strong reactions to the desert," he said. "But whatever your feelings for it, the desert does not change. It is dangerous whether you love it or hate it."

The clear attempt at intimidation irritated her. He might as well have said, *I am dangerous whether you love me or hate me.*

And I've done both, Desi told him silently. *But no more. I got though having any feeling for you a long time ago.*

"Funny, so is the Arctic," she said aloud, because two could play at the innuendo game. "Would it be better to freeze to death, or fry, do you think?"

His mouth tightened. "It is better to survive."

For a moment the scar showed white against the skin drawn tight over his cheekbone. It traced a path to above his ear and was lost in the thick black hair under his *keffiyeh*.

"And I guess you'd know," she said.

Salah's been wounded. For one unguarded moment she relived the overwhelming anguish that had hit her with those words. She was astonished to discover how shaken she was by the evidence of how close he had come to death. Her hand ached suddenly, as if with the need to touch. But she wasn't here to soothe any hurt of Salah's.

"Yes," he agreed.

As they reached the end of the corridor a uniformed guard, clasping a fist to his chest in salute, opened the door for them. Salah paused to issue instructions to him as Desi passed through into blinding sunlight.

She stopped. "My bags!"

Salah continued without pausing. "Come," was all he said, and his burnous streamed out behind him like a king's cloak as he stepped out into the hot desert wind.

The heat smacked her, a living thing. Desi stopped to take her first breath of the dry, orange-scented air with its tang of plane diesel.

And suddenly here she was. The place he had promised to bring her, ten long years ago. The place she had dreamt of, yearned for—believed would be her home. The desert, he had assured her, where men were men, where life was lived and love was loved with the deepest intensity. Where passion was a part of nature and human nature.

Where his passion for her would never die.

How many times, under his urgent, loving guidance, had she visualized herself in the desert, and how often, long after it was hopeless, had she wished and pleaded for life to have worked out differently! Begged fate to allow her to retrace the steps that had taken her away from that life with him. Ten long years on, she was here.

And she would give a year of her life to be anywhere else.

"So *hot!*" she cried, trying to shake the feeling. "It's only ten o'clock!"

"This is not a good time for foreigners in Central Barakat," Salah said.

"By *foreigners* do you mean any foreigner? Or just me?"

"Are you so different from ordinary people, Desi? Has fame made you weak?" he asked, but didn't wait for an answer. "Not many foreigners come at this time of year, unless to work in the oil fields. Next month will be cooler."

Next month would be too late. *It'll be hell on earth, Desi, but if you don't go now, I'm lost.* She would never forget the mixture of rage, grief and exhaustion in Sami's voice, the voice of a woman driven to the edge, fighting not to go over.

She glanced at Salah, wondering again how a boy of such passion as she remembered in him could have turned into a man ready to contemplate what he was now contemplating. But his face was closed, impossible to read.

Ten years ago she had understood every expression as it crossed his face. Now he was unreadable. As well read stone. What had done this to him? His injury? War itself?

A white limousine hummed in quiet readiness at the bottom of the steps. A chauffeur in black trousers, white polo shirt and a headscarf like Salah's leapt out to open the passenger door. As she slipped inside with Salah, an airport official arrived, carrying the two battered leather satchels that had accompanied her around the world over the past ten years. They were stowed in the trunk, doors banged, and the limo moved off.

And suddenly she was the last place in the world she would ever have chosen to be again: alone in a small space with Salah.

Two

At the height of the heat wave, Desi's father had accompanied her to Vancouver on a two-day modelling gig. Hating to miss one moment of time shared with Salah, she would have cancelled the engagement if she'd dared, and in the stifling heat of the city, she had wondered, not for the first time, why her friends envied her. She missed Salah with a desperate intensity, and could not wait to get back to the island. When they returned, it was Salah who met them at the ferry dock.

"Your mother is a little sick with the heat," Salah explained, but when he looked at her, Desi knew. The knowledge was like chain lightning in her blood, striking out from her heart again and again, every time she thought of it: he had to come. He couldn't wait even the extra half hour to see her.

"It has not rained since you left," he told her, and Desi's heart kicked with what he meant.

"You'll want to tell Salah all about your trip," her father

said, with masterly tact, or, more likely, masterly insensitivity. So she got in the front with Salah while her father sat in the back reading the local paper. But they did not talk much. There was a killing awareness between them, so powerful she felt she might explode with it.

The tarmac was practically steaming in the heat, as if it would melt the tires, and when they turned onto the unpaved road that led to the cottage dust billowed up around them in an impenetrable cloud.

"Like my country," Salah said. "Like the desert." And Desi half closed her eyes and dreamed that they were there, that he was driving her across the desert to his home.

"I wish I could see it," she whispered. "It must be so beautiful, the desert."

"Yes, beautiful. Like you."

He might as well have punched her in the stomach. She had never dreamed love would be like this, gasping for air, every cell of her body ready to burst.

"Am I?"

"I will take you to see it one day," he promised. "Then you will know how beautiful you are."

"Yes," she said softly, and they looked into each other's eyes and it was as if the promise were sealed with a kiss.

The kiss came later, as they sat on the dock, wet from swimming, watching as the sunset behind the trees painted the lake a rich gold.

"In my country I will show you an ocean of sand," he said. "The shadows at sunset are purple and blue. And every day it is different, because the wind—what do you say?—makes it into shapes."

"Sculpts," she offered.

"Sculpts, yes. In the desert the wind is a sculptor. I wish I were a sculptor, Desi," he breathed, and his hand moved up to explore the line of her temple, cheek, chin, and then slipped behind her neck under the wet hair.

It was her first kiss, and it was unbelievably, piercingly sweet. It assailed her body as though a thousand tender mouths touched her everywhere at once. With Salah bending over her, their mouths fused, she melted down onto the dock, and the sun-warmed weathered wood against her back added its mite to the overwhelming sensation that poured through her.

Her hand lifted of its own volition to the warm skin of his chest, his shoulder, and a moment later Salah lifted his mouth to look at her. His face was gold and shadow, the most beautiful thing she had ever seen. They gazed into each other's eyes.

"Desi, I love you," he said; she breathed, "I love you, Salah," and all around them was perfection.

She had never seen real desert so close before. Mountains and sea were her natural background; from her childhood she had never questioned the rightness of that.

Until now. Now, as she watched an eternity of dusky sand pass, smoky tendrils of longing and belonging reached out from the stark landscape into the vehicle, into her being, her self, and clasped her heart.

"So," Salah said, in a harsh voice that immediately brought her back to the now. "So, Desi, you come to my country at last."

She could feel her emotions rising to the bait, and fought down the impulse to rake over their ten-year-old history.

"Well, I guess you could…"

"After ten years, what have you to say to me?"

"I didn't ask you to meet me, and I've nothing to say to you," she said, forgetting Sami, forgetting everything except basic life-saving procedures.

"You lie. What do you come for, if not this?"

This?

"What are you talking about?" she demanded.

He looked at her for an electric moment, his eyes blazing as if he were struggling against some powerful impulse, and she held her breath and awaited the outcome.

"You know what I mean."

She licked her lips. "Didn't your father tell you why I'm here?"

Salah snorted. "My father's work! Even the immigration official knew better than to believe it. Why do you come to me now? What do you want? What do you hope I can give you? You are too late."

She couldn't believe this. What was Time, then? Ten years since they had spoken, but here they were, picking up the argument as if scarcely an hour had passed.

"I don't want anything from you! Who told you I wanted—?"

He pulled her sunglasses off, flinging them down on the seat between them.

"Do not hide behind darkness and tell me lies."

"What do you think you're doing?" she grabbed the glasses up again, fumbling to unfold them.

"When women veil their hair it is to protect their modesty. When they veil their eyes it is to conceal deceit."

It was impossible to put the glasses back on, after that, impossible to leave them off. She glared at him, anger rising in her.

"And when men accuse women it's to avoid facing their own guilt. What do *you* want?"

"We will discover. But I did not go to you, Desi. You came to me."

"That's a Napoleonic ego you're nursing there, Salah. I came to your *country*."

The flesh on his face tightened. "To visit my father," he said, measuring every word.

"Exactly!" she said. "I think we're back where you started, aren't we?"

He was not fazed.

"Why do you deny it? There is no shame in returning to your first love when other men are unsatisfactory. If your first love has waited for you, all is well."

"Do you have any idea how pompous you sound?"

"Do you regret our unmatched passion, Desi?" His black eyes burned into hers. "That day in the cabin—do you remember it? What could ever reach it, if we lived a thousand years? Is that why you are here?"

The memory of that summer welled up in her at his words. Heat burned her blood. That incredible, bone deep, never-to-be-repeated yearning for the touch of another human being—it was as if she had sat by a fire she thought was ashes and dust, and with one measured kick he had set it roaring into an inferno again.

"I regretted it for a while," she said. "And then not. What about you?"

"Your hair," he said. "I want to see your hair."

Her head twitched back. "Don't touch me!"

"Ten years."

She could not prevent him. He reached out to grasp the brim of her hat and slowly pulled it off. At his bidding, the ash-blond hair came tumbling down around her shoulders. It was like being undressed by any other man.

"Still the colour of the desert at the edge of the mountains."

One strong finger reached for a lock, curled around it. He had said it ten years ago. *Not the golden sand you see on post-cards, Desi,* he had whispered as they lay in each other's arms, and he kissed a lock of her hair, *more beautiful than that. The colour before sunset, just where it flows into purple foothills. I will show you.*

Her skin shivered with unbearable sensation. He was watching her with half-lidded hawk eyes, the better to see her with. She lifted her chin to draw back, and could not.

Time, the great trickster, stopped altogether then, and they stared at each other, unmoving, his hand locked in her hair, her eyes wide, hypnotized. Outside the car, blinding sun and a harsh, unforgiving landscape. Inside, the unforgiving landscape of the heart.

The car went over a bump, kicking time into motion again. Desi lifted her hand and pulled her hair from his grasp.

"Don't touch me," she began, but even as she spoke the command his control snapped. One strong dark hand clamped her wrist and his other arm went around her waist to pull her into his embrace, thigh to thigh, breast to chest, her hands helpless, her body arcing against him as if in erotic submission.

For a moment they were frozen there, eyes fixed on each other's face, but if it was the past she was yearning for, there was nothing of the tender boy she remembered in the angry blackness of a gaze that seemed to swallow her every attempt at conscious thought, fatally weakening her resistance.

At last she found the use of her hands and lifted to push them against his shoulders. Still he held her, resisting the pressure with frightening ease. His *keffiyeh* fell forward over one shoulder, cocooning them in their own little world.

Their own world. It had always been their own world.

"Salah!" she protested, but the name was lost in a gasp as his lips took possession of hers.

His mouth was strong and hungry, and her body heat went instantly to melting point as the kiss devoured her. Need like a starving child rose up in her then, an ancient, unfamiliar yearning—hunger, and thirst, and the bone-deep ache of a decade bursting a heart that had been locked tight against feeling for too long.

Terrified by the force of her anguished need, gasping at her overwhelming response, she resisted the powerful urge to wrap her arms around his neck and drink deep of what she had been deprived of so long, and instead struggled and pushed against him, dragging her parched mouth away from water in the desert, fighting against instinct and compulsion like one who knows the source of all they need is poisoned.

He lifted his mouth at last. Again they were still, staring into each other's eyes at point blank range, her hair flowing over his arm, his black gaze over her face.

"I always liked to taste my name on your lips," he remembered.

Something like panic gripped her. "Let me go."

Salah breathed as if for ammunition in the battle for self-control, and opened his arms. She flung herself back indignantly, flicking her hair, tweaking her clothes straight, avoiding looking at him for fear of what he could read in her eyes.

With all her heart she wanted to avoid confrontation, pretend this had never happened. But it would be fatal to let it pass. At last she could raise her eyes and stare at him.

"If you kiss me again I will hit you," she said between her teeth.

"Beware of chain reactions, then."

His voice was like iced gravel. A thrill of something that was not quite fear went through her.

"Can we leave it out?" she cried. "I've been flying for most of a day and I'm tired!"

He nodded, lifted up and opened a briefcase, pulled out some papers, and began to study them. Suddenly he was the stranger again, in the unfamiliar *keffiyeh* and desert robes. He looked like an oil sheikh.

Just like that, it seemed, he could dismiss her from his consciousness. Desi resisted the sudden, mad urge to go for him and tear off the intimidating headgear, as if that would restore him to the boy she had known.

But there was more than a *keffiyeh* between this chiselled, haughty face and the Salah she'd once overwhelmingly loved.

Three

Perhaps if her parents had been more awake to what was going on, Desi's personal disaster might have been averted. But the house was at peak capacity, with every bed full, and in the heat there seemed to be twice as much work, with guests demanding fresh towels, cold drinks, and extra service.

They had a retreat, a place that the children had used as a hideaway for years: under the old wooden pier that lay on one side of the lake a few hundred yards from the house. Every summer Desi and her brother dragged an air mattress underwater and up onto the rocks beneath, and then inflated it so that it lay half floating, half moored.

They called it their clubhouse. Sometimes, when avoiding household chores or ignoring mealtimes, the children had hidden there, giggling and listening to their mother call.

In sunlit hours, the spot was pleasantly shady. In rain, they could pretend it was dry. And in the evening it was perfection to sit there with a small smudge coil keeping the mosquitoes at bay, talking about life, death and destiny, and what they would do when they grew up.

Salah and Desi spent many hours there that summer, away from the paying guests who wandered up and down at the lake's edge. In the searing heat, it was pleasant to lie there, while shafts of burning light pierced the gloom, the air mattress bumping lightly against the sides of the pier or the rocks as the water lapped. In the evenings they lay in each other's embrace, watching as stars and moon appeared.

With her head resting on his shoulder, his fingers threading her hair, they dreamed together about the future. They would get married as soon as she finished high school. She would move to the Barakat Emirates to be with him, and make her life there. They would have four children, two boys and two girls.

Neither Salah nor Desi meant for it to happen, though it was always Salah who drew back, when Desi was too much in love, and too drowned in sensation, to know where the point of no return was.

"We have time, Desi," Salah would say gently. "All our lives. We can wait." And of course she agreed.

But everything seemed to conspire against this determined nobility: the heat, their innocence, and the fact that they were always together, so often alone.

It was there under the dock, when he told her about the war in Parvan, that their control finally broke.

Brave little Parvan, which had been invaded by the Kaljuks, and had long been fighting an unequal war with little help from its friends. Prince Omar of Central Barakat had formed a company of Cup Companions and joined the war on the side of Prince Kavian of Parvan.

"The Kaljuks are monsters," Salah told her. "Prince Omar

is right—we can't let them do what they are doing to Parvan. He is right to join the fight."

Desi's heart choked with a sudden presentiment of doom.

"You—*you* wouldn't go, would you?"

"My father has forbidden me, he says I must finish one year of university first. He thinks the war will be over this winter. The Kaljuks are tired and Parvan will never give up. But if it is not—what else can I do, Desi? I must join the Prince. I must help them."

Tears starting in her eyes, she begged him not to go to war. She pleaded her love and their future. The life together they would never have if he were killed. Those four children who would never be born.

"Marry me now, Desi," he said roughly, drawing her in against his chest and holding her tight. "Then, if I die, I will leave you with a son to take care of you when he grows up. Come home with me! Marry me now!"

He kissed her then, when all their barriers were down. And amid the perfect silence of nature, that silence that is wind and birdsong and still water, they could no longer say no to the wild desire in their blood.

She always marvelled, afterwards, at the coincidence. After two weeks of utter joy, of living in their own secret, magic world, on the night before Salah's departure, her brother Harry arrived for the weekend bringing a magazine.

"Baby, it's you!" he said proudly, opening it to show them all something that the family was still a long way from being used to: a full page ad with Desi's photo.

It had been her first high-fashion assignment, shot in Toronto months before, and it had been a very different world from any she had experienced up till then. Desi had been awed by the arrogance of the makeup artist, never mind the photographer, who everyone said was the absolute best…

The results, too, were different: the peak of professional skill evident in the ad, which was all in shades of bronze. Desi sat on a director's chair with her feet sprawled wide, her knees angled in, in a trench coat, buttoned and belted, but exposing a V of sensual dark lace at both breast and hip. With her elbow resting on the arm of the chair, propping up her chin, Desi gazed at the viewer with limpid beauty. Between her feet was a fabulous leather handbag. Glossy shoes matched the bag.

The family and guests crowded round. "You look absolutely stunning!"

"Oooh, very sexy!"

"I'll buy one! Just show me the money!"

Everybody was delighted, thrilled for her. Only one voice was silent. Desi looked shyly up at Salah, expecting his proud approval.

His face was dark with shock.

"They exploit you," he said quietly, and it was a terrible slap, all the worse because it was public. The babble in the room damped down as Desi gasped and blushed bright red.

"*Exploit* me? Do you know how much I was paid for that shoot?" she cried indignantly. "And the hotel where they put us up…"

"They put you up in a fine hotel and pay you to expose yourself," Salah said.

"Expose? My *legs!*" she cried. "Everybody does it! I'm not nude, you know!"

"Yes," he said. And it was true that the positioning of the bag between her feet, with the innocent vulnerability in her eyes, was disturbingly erotic.

For once her mother rose to the occasion.

"Isn't it wonderful the differences you still find in cultural perceptions, when we're all so worried about American monoculture sweeping the world?" she said, picking up the magazine and flipping it shut. "Congratulations, darling, we'll look at it again later. It's a cold supper tonight, everyone, shall we eat now?"

Tears blinding her, Desi got up and banged out through the screen door into the star-filled night. The door banged a second time behind her, but she did not stop running.

He caught up with her down by the water's edge.

"Desi!"

"Why did you do that? Why did you humiliate me in front of everyone?" she demanded.

"If you are humiliated, it is not me. That picture, Desi—"

"Oh, shut up! Shut up! There is nothing wrong with that picture! It's a fashion shoot! I was *so* lucky to get that job, girls wait years for something like that! It'll open so many doors for me!"

That was her agent talking. The truth was that modelling, the teenage girl's fantasy, had never really been Desi's dream. Perhaps it was the impact of her parents' ideals on her, her island upbringing, for what she had seen of the life so far she did not like. But, perversely human, when pressed, she defended what she did not believe in.

"Desi, we are going to be married. You will be my wife. You can't pose like this for other men."

"Men?" she cried. "That's not a men's magazine! It's fashion! It's for *women!* I'm advertising a *handbag!*"

"No," he said levelly. "You advertise sex."

He had the outsider's clarity, but it was too much to expect that she could see what he saw, or that he would understand the intimate connection between sex and sales.

"You don't know what you're talking about!"

"Desi, one picture is not important. But this work you do— will it all be like that? Is this what a modelling career means?"

"All like *what,* for heaven's sake? I was fully dressed! Wait for it, Salah, next month I'll be in an *underwear* catalogue! What is your problem?"

"Desi, a Muslim woman cannot do such things. It is impossible."

She was silent, listening to the crickets. Then, "I'm not a Muslim woman," she said slowly.

"Desi!" he pleaded.

She burst into tears. "And if that's what it means—that my photograph is seen as disgusting, then…and if that's what *you* think—if that's what *you* see when you look at that picture of me…oh, God, you make me feel like a…like a…"

They were too young to see that what had motivated his outburst was not religion, but jealousy. Sexual possessiveness.

"And if you're so high and holy, Salah, what about what we've been doing? How does that stack up with your principles?"

"We love each other. We are going to be married!" he said, but she thought she could see doubt in his eyes.

She said accusingly, "You think what we're doing is wrong, don't you?"

"No, Desi!"

She cringed down to the bottom of her soul.

"Oh, *God!* That is so *sick!*"

If he felt guilty about their lovemaking, what did that mean about how he saw her? Shame swept through her. And the stupid fragile dream she'd been dreaming cracked and split open, and the real world was there, beyond the jagged edges, telling her she'd been a fool.

Suddenly she was saying terrible things to him, accusing him of tricking her into sex, and then judging her for giving in. Horrible things that she did not believe, but was somehow driven to say.

His face grew white as he listened, and then Salah erupted with things about the corrupt West which he did not believe and always argued against with friends at home.

Corrupt. The word hung in the air between them as they stared at each other, bewildered, their hearts raw with hurt, and far too young to make sense of what was happening.

"You mean me!" she cried then. "Well, if I'm corrupt, you're the corrupter! I hate you!" She whirled and ran back into the house and up to her room.

She locked her bedroom door, and buried her head under the duvet, trying to drown out the sound of pebbles hitting her window during the night, the whispered pleadings at her door.

She did not come down again until after breakfast the next morning, just in time to say a cool goodbye to Salah, with all the others, before her father took him to the ferry. As he got into the car he looked at her with the reproach of a dying stag who cannot understand what has motivated his killer.

Salah never came to the island again.

Four

The palace clung to a rocky slope above the winding river and the city between, brooding over the scene like a dream of white, terra cotta and blue. From the plane, in all the glory of its dome and its arched terraces, the palace had looked like something out of a fairy tale, but approached from below it had the air of a fortress.

It was some time before she understood that they *were* approaching it. They drove through the centre of the city, past the bustle of a market, through a small herd of reluctant goats driven by a grinning urchin, then along wide streets bordered on two sides with high white walls topped with greenery. So entranced was she with the unfamiliar sights that it was only after they left these walls behind that she realized there was only the palace ahead.

"Where are we going?" she asked, when the answer was already obvious.

The car stopped at a gate and the chauffeur exchanged words through the window with an armed guard.

Salah put the papers away, snapped the briefcase shut and set it aside. After a moment, as if at a thought, he reached out and spun the locks. She felt it like a slap.

"You can never be too sure," she said sarcastically. "But really, the state secrets of little Barakat are safe from me."

He looked at her with a black gaze that revealed nothing.

"What is this place, Salah?"

"It is Prince Omar's palace."

"Am I staying *here?*"

"What else? Should I put you up in a hotel? Do you think I forget what I owe your family?"

"Won't I be meeting your family?"

They moved up the incline, past an unmanned sentry post, then under a broad archway and into a courtyard where there were several parked vehicles.

"Except for my father, who is at the dig, my family go to the mountains in summer. The heat is bad for my mother's health. Only the poor remain in the city in summer, and they move down by the river."

His eyes were hard. She remembered the very different look in his eyes the last time they had met, on the morning that he left the island for the last time.

Never got over her? On the contrary, the boy who had loved her had disappeared. He was changed out of all recognition. *You had a lucky escape!* she told herself.

Her heart, contrarily, mourned a loss.

"So why are *you* still in the city?"

He lifted one corner of his mouth and looked at her as if she were being naive.

"You stayed in the city to meet me? Why? What do you want?"

"Not what I want, Desi. What you want."

He opened his door as two servants appeared through a doorway. The men seized her bags from the trunk and disappeared. The chauffeur opened her door. The heat slapped her again as she got out.

"What has it got to do with me?"

"I will be your guide to my father's dig. Did you not expect it?"

Of course Salah will be your guide. The entire plan depended on this, and yet, somehow…not until this moment had Desi really believed that it was going to happen. That she'd be travelling across the desert for hours with only Salah for company….

Her eyes hurt as she gazed at him, as if they were letting in too much sun.

"Well, I'm sorry. Your father said, a guide. I didn't expect…"

"No?" his manifest disbelief infuriated her, even though he was right.

"I'm sorry, but this is the only time I've got. It's when I normally go to the island."

The word was electric between them.

"And the case is so urgent," he said.

There was no answer she could make to that, without looking even more of a selfish idiot. She turned her head to escape his cynic's gaze, and a panel of exquisite, ancient tilework met her eyes.

She had stayed in some pretty fabulous places in her time: a hot modelling career opened a lot of doors. But not so far an active royal palace. Never a place with such an aura of power, past and present.

"Will I get to meet them?" she asked. She knew that Prince Omar and Princess Jana had children of their own, as well as two daughters from Omar's first marriage.

Salah led her under a worn, intricately arabesqued stone archway onto a tiled path.

"They go to Lake Parvaneh in summer. Princess Jana asked me to assure you of your welcome here, and apologizes for her absence."

He opened a door and ushered her along a path bordering a formal garden and thence into an internal courtyard so entrancing Desi stopped short and gasped.

Columns, floor, stairs and walls were covered with beautiful, intricately patterned mosaic tiling. A perfectly still reflecting pool in the centre reflected greenery and sunlight and the balcony above, with a mirror's clarity and water's depth. Cloisters ran around the walls on all sides; an ancient tree rose up in one corner, its gnarled branches and thick leaves shading the space from the morning sun. More tumbled greenery cascaded down from the balcony, or entwined the tall columns and latticework.

It was compellingly beautiful, deeply restful. The temperature seemed to have dropped by at least ten degrees. Desi heaved a sigh of sheer wonder.

"Isn't it spectacular!"

"It is more beautiful in spring, with the flowers," said Salah and, pausing under the archway, he threw a switch.

She heard a rumble, a groan, as if some great underground creature had been disturbed in its rest, and then the perfect reflection in the water shimmered and was lost as fountains leapt up into the air from the centre of the pool.

The fine spray damped her face as she stood smiling up at the vision.

"Now, that's what I call air conditioning!" Her spirits lifted and she laughed for sheer pleasure.

Watching as the fine mist damped her lips, as if a kiss had moistened them, his face closed. He turned away to lead her through the spray up a flight of stairs and along the balcony.

A sudden gust caught his cloak and it billowed around him, the image of the hero in an ancient tale. Desi was struck by the same promise of timelessness and belonging that the sands had whispered to her, as if they had met here a thousand years ago....

He opened a door.

She stopped to catch her breath again at the doorway. It was a magnificent room, huge, but divided into comfortable niches by the artistic use of rugs, furniture clusters, and intricately carved antique room dividers in cedar, ebony and sandalwood.

Above the doorway and windows, panels of stained glass threw patterns of coloured sunlight onto the white-painted walls. Fat brocade cushions forming sofas and armchairs were interspersed with low tables; on the walls above hung fabulous paintings and patterned mirrors, with niches holding burnished bronze plates and pitchers that glowed like gold. Covering the dark polished wood floor was the biggest silk carpet she had seen outside a museum. A Chinese cabinet looked as if it had been painted for an emperor.

The plates and jars that glowed like gold, she realized with a jolt, were gold.

A sweeping arch gave onto a farther room, and against the opposite wall a soft breeze coming through the jalousies of an open window disturbed the silk canopy of a low bed whose pillows and spread were patterned in turquoises and purples.

The luxury was suddenly and profoundly erotic. So different from the bed under the old dock ten years ago, but pulsating with sensual and sexual promise. As if that other bed, those places they had made their bed, had been a foreshadowing, a dream of which this, now, was the living, breathing, full-colour reality.

They stood gazing at each other, locked in the moment, as the tentacles of memory reached out from the thing called *bed* and began to entwine them.

She had thought herself immune. She had imagined that hatred had blanked out the love that had once consumed her, and that in the intervening years indifference had wiped out hatred.

Desire, it seemed, was independent of such considerations. It operated outside them, it must, because right now his eyes were as hot on her skin as the desert sun.

Desi thought wildly, with a kind of panic, *if he kissed me now…*

A woman appeared silently, suddenly, as if from nowhere, and murmured a greeting. Salah drew in a controlled breath, spoke a few words to her, and when he turned back to Desi all sign that he had been affected by the moment was blanked out behind obsidian shutters.

"I have a meeting now. Fatima speaks a little English. She will look after you and bring you lunch later. It will be best if you remain in the palace today. We will have dinner about sunset. Do you wish something to eat or drink now? Fatima will bring it."

"Nothing, thanks. Do you live in the palace?" she asked, not sure which answer she was hoping for.

"I have rooms here, yes," he said. "We all do."

"'We'?"

"Prince Omar's Cup Companions have offices and apartments in the palace."

Desi remembered all about the Cup Companions. In ancient times holders of the title had had duties no more onerous than to carouse with the monarch and take his mind off affairs of state.

"Now they work very hard," Salah had told her, that day he confided his dreams of one day serving with Prince Omar.

"They are the Prince's working cabinet. One day, *inshallah,* I will achieve this—to work with Prince Omar."

I don't know what Salah's exact mandate is, but my brothers have heard he's in Prince Omar's confidence, Sami had explained more recently. *They're convinced he's very very VIP.*

"We heard about your appointment, of course. Congratulations, Salah, I know it was always your dream," she said now. "Your parents must be proud."

"*Mash'allah,*" he said dismissively. *It was God's will.*

In another life, he would have come to her first with the news.

Looking up at the shuttered face, the arrogant tilt of his chin, the hanging judge's eyes, Desi could well believe that Salah had a Prince's ear. But she herself wouldn't marry him now for all the power and influence in six continents. She was suddenly violently, intensely glad she'd agreed to help Samiha. Marriage to Salah would be a hell of a life.

Five

"They want me to marry Salah," Samiha had said.

The harassment had begun during the last year of her undergraduate degree, after Sami's father had been killed in a work accident. With his death, her eldest brother, Walid, became "head of the family". The trouble started almost immediately, and because her mother caved in under the pressure, Sami had had to give in. First she had been forced to wear the head covering called *hejab* whenever she was out of the house. Other restrictions followed, in a steady erosion of her freedom.

But when Walid, supported by their brother Arif, started to suggest that the headscarf was not sufficient to protect her from men's lusts or show her devotion to their religion, and that Sami really ought to wear *niqab*, the full face veil, Sami had finally found the courage to introduce him to Farid, her fiancé. The couple hoped that Walid would be happy to pass his troublesome ownership of his sister to a husband.

This had been a tactical error. The secrecy of it, her brazen determination to make her own choice, outraged Walid. It violated his right as her protector and guide to choose a good husband for her. Farid al Muntazer, though a Muslim, did not meet with his approval.

Samiha should marry someone from back home. Someone connected to them. Family.

"But Salah's your *cousin!*" Desi had protested, scandalized.

In her distress, Sami had turned to Desi as naturally as breathing. They no longer lived on the same street, but there were ways of keeping in touch that were almost as good as walking home from school together. Wherever Desi was in the world, the two friends always spent a couple of hours a week on the phone.

"All the better!" Sami informed her bitterly. "The old ways are best, you see!"

"They're crazy! Sami, you can't give in to this!" The idea filled her with primitive horror. Sami and Salah, married? It couldn't be allowed! "You're twenty-seven! It's none of their business who you marry. You've got to refuse!"

"I am refusing. But my mother is being very weak. My brothers keep telling me how lucky I am, can you believe it? Salah's got everything—he's rich, handsome, Prince Omar's right hand man."

"I don't care if he's Prince Omar himself, he's your cousin!"

"If he were Prince Omar himself, Des, he wouldn't be my cousin."

"That's what they call gallows humour, is it?"

"I knew there was a word for it."

"What can you do to make your refusal stick?"

"I know what I can't do. I can't marry anyone but Farid. I'll drink bleach first. But Walid is pretty crazy right now, and Arif is right behind him. Full-frontal confrontation is probably not a good idea."

"Can you just tell Salah himself? He must think you want this. Surely if he knew—"

"Maybe, but, Des, I'm actually scared to risk it. I don't know what *his* reasons are. Maybe he needs a Canadian passport or something."

"*What?* He's a Cup Companion! Why would he need—"

"Des, I can't risk telling Salah!" Sami protested in a tight voice. "I don't know what's in it for him! If he told Walid…"

"Do you really think Salah would—"

"I don't know who to trust!" Sam cried, and Desi suddenly realized how close her friend was to outright panic. When your own brothers could turn rabid, what was safe?

"Oh, I feel so useless! I wish I could help!"

"Des, you're the only one who can."

Her heart had started to pound right there. "*Me?* What—"

"It's no good challenging the noble protectors of Islamic purity head on. I figure I have to start from the other end."

"I'd be very happy to kneecap them both for you, Sam, but I think it's actually illegal."

"Not that end."

Desi's heart seemed to feel she was trying for the thousand metre world record.

"You want me to kneecap…Salah?"

"That's the one! Do you think Salah ever got over you, Desi?"

"Yes," she said crisply. "Without a doubt. In ten years he hasn't lifted a finger in my direction."

"He hasn't married, either."

"Clearly the women of Central Barakat are not stupid."

"I don't think he ever really got over you. And that was then. Look at you now. Did you see what *Everywoman* called you this week? Hang on a sec, I've actually got it here." There was the sound of rustling paper, then Sami started reading.

"'Perhaps the most iconically beautiful of all the supermodels on the world scene today, Desirée Drummond—Desi to everyone caught in the intimacy of that smile—projects the haunting vulnerability of a woman who has never learned to hide her heart.'"

"How wrong can one sentence be?" said Desi.

"Whatever reasons Salah's got for wanting the marriage, I bet if he thought he stood any chance with you…"

"Along the lines of an icicle's chance in hell…"

"…he'd walk away from this deal so fast we'd see smoke at his heels."

The bottom fell out of Desi's stomach. She tried to laugh.

"Sami, I haven't seen Salah in ten years!"

"Yeah, but he's seen you! Your face is everywhere, isn't it? You can bet *he* hasn't forgotten."

Her face on a magazine cover would only serve to remind him of why he'd rejected her, but Desi couldn't embark on that now.

"You aren't dating anyone, are you? I wouldn't ask if you were involved with someone. At least—I hope I wouldn't," Sami admitted with disarming honesty.

"Are you joking me, Sam?"

"Des, all you'd have to do is—let him think there's a chance. Talk about those carefree summers on the island. Remind him how you used to hero-worship him. You know you can do it."

Desi took a deep breath, and reminded herself that Sami hadn't been there. And afterwards she'd told no one, not even Sami, all of it.

"Oh, Sam…" she began pleadingly.

"Des, I know it's a terrible thing to ask. But this is the rest of my life, and you're my only hope. Just think if your father wanted to force you to marry—Allan, say."

Her cousin Allan was a blameless stockbroker in Toronto, but Desi shuddered.

"I understand. You know I understand. But honestly, Sam—"

"All we need is some excuse for you to visit Central Barakat. Could you be looking for locations or something?"

"Models don't scout locations. Anyway, even if I did visit, why should I run into Salah? The country's not that small."

"After all your family did for him all those years! Of course you'd get in touch and ask for his help! Wouldn't you?"

"When pigs fly," Desirée said grimly.

"But why? Of course you'd call him! Harry did, when he was over there. Salah treated him like royalty, he told me."

"Sam, if I did go, if I did see him, it wouldn't do any good. Ashes are ashes. They don't stay warm for ten years."

"They do. Salah used to act as if…"

She would not ask. She didn't care how he used to act.

"As if what?" Desi blurted.

"As if his heart was broken, I guess. For years when I mentioned your name he'd stiffen, the way people do when they're protecting a sore spot."

"I'd be happy to think Salah suffered, but I think it was probably gas."

"Hey—that's it!" Sami said. "Two birds with one stone! Think of how sweet revenge would taste."

"It's tempting to consider myself a worthy successor to Sharon Stone, but come on, Sam!"

The wind went out of Sami's sails abruptly.

"You're right. It's crazy of me to ask. Sorry, sorry. But, Desi, what can I do? Tell me what to do!" And again, the flame of desperation was there, licking around the edges of her voice. Desi's heart contracted.

"God, Sam—can't you and Farid just elope?"

"Walid is not above making threats. Maybe—probably he'd do nothing, but you know I can't count on that."

"Making threats? That's disgusting!" Desi exclaimed. "Is Walid completely insane?"

"Don't get me started."

"What about talking to your Uncle Khaled?" Uncle Khaled was her father's younger brother, and since her father's death, Sami had explained, was the head of the extended family. Uncle Khaled was also Salah's father.

"I've thought of that. But Uncle Khaled and Aunt Arwa are really keen on me and Salah. They've told my mother they're thrilled. So I can't just ask Uncle Khaled straight out, either, because if that went wrong… But, Des, if you were there you could sound him out for me—"

Sami broke off with a gasp. "Oh, *Allah,* I've got it! I've got it!" she cried. "Uncle Khaled's dig!"

Six

The servant led her through the palace to the foot of an external staircase running up to a large terrace backed by the dome, and left her. Desi went slowly up, gazing entranced as the vista was slowly revealed.

The sun was just disappearing behind the horizon of deep-purple desert on the right, pulling a cloak of fiery, furnace-red sky after it; to the left the last of its rays caught the mountain tops with liquid gold. Below and beyond the palace the city was lighting up, a swathe of glittering jewels cut in two by the darkness of the great river that carved its way from the mountains to the sea. As the sun's last light faded, the tree-lined river began to reflect the myriad lights from its banks.

Desi drew a long breath as she arrived at the top and sighed it out. Magic.

Salah was standing halfway along the terrace, looking out over the city. He turned, and at once she was locked by his gaze. Desi put one foot in front of the other and, as helpless as if a magnet were drawing her, slowly moved towards where he waited.

Her hair was loose, he saw, caressing shoulders and neck; her skin was without a flaw. She was wearing sea-blue silk that turned her chameleon eyes to turquoise: a clingy slip top bared the smooth skin of her throat and the shadow between her breasts; flowing trousers caressed the tantalizing shape of hip, thigh and leg when she moved; a matching jacket, the collar standing up under her chin, showed purple and gold embroidery. Gold and amethyst glinted against her neck and ears. Her sandals were delicate straps of gold across her insteps.

But it was her eyes where the true beauty resided—that wide level gaze that once had shown him all the truth of her soul, the gentle sweep of mobile eyebrows under a broad, pale forehead. The curve of her cheeks like wind-sculpted sand, and the mouth—wide, full, sensuous. Her face had always held this contradiction, as if her eyes held no awareness of the sensuality promised by her mouth and body.

Long ago, he had awakened something else in that gaze. Joy, sensual gratitude and love had mixed in a gaze for him and him alone. He had believed he was the only one to see it.

Falsely, as it happened, for it was exploited by every advertiser she posed for. But men had been fools before him, and would be fools when he was dust.

And still in ten long years he had not seen beauty to match it. But he would not fall victim to that beauty again. He had been weak earlier, but he would be that much more on his guard now.

Her gaze was guarded, her beauty remote. But something more: in her eyes was more than a simple veiling of the inner. She was lying to him.

What lie? Well, he would find out.

"Good evening, Desi," he said.

He had dispensed with the *keffiyeh* and the oil sheikh's robes. Now he was wearing flowing cream cotton trousers and a knee-length shirt, the outfit called *shalwar kamees*. The shirt was open at the neck and rolled up at the wrists, leaving his dark throat and his forearms bare. His head, too, was bare, black curls kissed into gold by the setting sun.

Without the *keffiyeh,* he was less a stranger. She looked up into the harsh face, searching for traces of the fresh-faced boy she had loved, and wondered if he, too, were looking for the awkward, naive girl of ten years ago.

The boy was gone forever. The eyes she remembered could never have looked at her as these eyes did: hard and suspicious, even as they raked her face with a hunger so blatant she shivered.

"It's a fabulous view," she said, to defuse the sudden tension. But his jaw only tightened. She felt a sudden jolt of heat against her back—his hand, guiding her.

They moved silently along the terrace and into a roof garden. In the centre of the space was a small fountain, its splashing sounds a caress to the ears in the twilight.

He led her to an alcove surrounded by trellis, enclosed in greenery, where a low platform was luxuriantly spread with carpets and pillows. He kicked off his sandals, stepped up onto the platform and sank down on the lush carpet amongst silken pillows.

Lying back against the cushions, dark and arrogant, he suddenly looked like a sultan in a storybook.

She hesitated, without knowing why. With a regal gesture he indicated the cushions opposite him in the little enclosure. Desi slipped off her own sandals, stepped up along the soft carpet and melted down into the luxuriously comfortable cushions opposite him.

"You are beautiful tonight." The words seemed choked, as if they came out in spite of his intentions.

He had said it before. *Tonight—and always,* he had said then.

"Mash'allah," she said, with a wry half smile. He had taught her the traditional Barakati response to a compliment. *Like crossing your fingers,* he'd said, *you have to avert the evil eye.*

His eyes darkened, suddenly, like a cat's, but his lips tightened, as if the fact that she used the expression gave him pleasure but he would not allow himself to feel it.

Beyond the trellis and greenery, sky and sunset created a backdrop of magnificence. Intimacy closed around them like a velvet paw, trapping them for the gods' amusement.

The desert was deep purple now in the darkness. A soft breeze lifted her hair as she gazed at the scene, tossed it lightly across her face. Shaking it back, Desi sighed in pure delight. A feeling of peace invaded her bones, and she searched for something innocuous to say. She did not want to fight with him.

"This must be the most unusual dining room in the world."

"Princess Jana designed it for private use. It is Omar's favourite retreat. No state business is ever conducted here."

"I hope food is coming soon! I haven't eaten since London, and I'm ravenous."

"I apologize. Fatima should have offered you lunch."

"She did. I wasn't hungry. Then."

"And you didn't eat on the plane?"

She shook her head. "I don't usually."

There was a curious amplified clicking noise, and then down in the city the haunting voice of the *muezzin* began to recite the call to prayer. The reciter's deep tones, half singing, half chanting, poured out over the city, echoing in the distance. They sat in silence, listening, trying not to remember how, long ago, he had lovingly described this sound to her....

A waiter came, spread a tablecloth on the platform between them and set down a couple of jugs and four goblets. He half-filled the goblets and disappeared again.

Allahu akhbar. Allahu akhbar. Hayya alas salaat.

"What is he saying?"

"God is great. Come to prayer," Salah translated softly.

"Curious to hear so many echoes! Does the desert do that?"

"Echoes?" A smile twitched one corner of his mouth and he shook his head. "Each mosque has its own *muezzin,* so that no one lives beyond reach of the call. Up here we hear them all."

The last note sounded as darkness covered the sky. Desi leaned back and looked up through the tracery of trellis and leaves at the stars just beginning to appear.

"This is magic," she breathed again, and then, with a little frown, "It reminds me of somewhere! What is it? That sky is pure velvet; I can't think when I last saw such a—*oh!*"

Heat burned up her chest and into her face like a flash fire, and she instinctively jerked upright.

"What is it?" Salah said.

"Nothing." She coughed unconvincingly. "Something in my throat."

"You are reminded of something? A place? A time?"

"No, not really." She coughed again and reached for a glass.

"Yes," he said harshly, as all his intentions for the evening went up in smoke. "The island. I, too, Desi. The first time I sat here under the trellis at night I remembered those nights under the dock. We looked up at stars glowing with endless beauty, telling us it was the right time, the right place, the right one."

Desi gazed at him, frozen, the glass halfway to her mouth.

"You remember, Desi?"

"Do I?" she asked bitterly. Tears were ripping at the back of her throat, but she was damned if she would give him that victory.

"Yes!" he said fiercely. His face was shadowed in the candlelight, his eyes hidden, his mouth hard. "Yes, you know how our love was! Tell me! I want to know that you remember."

"Why, since *you* forgot?"

"I thought the stars would die before my love for you. I told you that, didn't I? *When each of those stars is a blackened lump, my love will still be burning for you.* Isn't that what I told you?"

Her throat closed tight. She set the glass down again without drinking. "I don't remember," she said, her eyes shadowed and grey.

"Ah, that is well. Because I was wrong. My love did not last."

"No kidding. And are you proud of that fact? I've always wondered."

"Proud?" His eyes flashed. "Why should I be proud? I was shamed, for you and for me. My love did not die honourably, like a star, consuming itself in its own burning. You know how it died."

"Your love died because it was fantasy from day one. The stars going out? It wouldn't have withstood a hiccup."

The waiter appeared out of the night, shocking them both into silence, and set down a basket of bread and another filled with sprigs of greenery before disappearing again.

"Tonight," he said, "they will bring us the foods I told you of, in those starry nights when we lived a dream."

She closed her eyes and breathed for calm as memory smote her. "Why?"

"Because it was a promise. A man keeps his promises," he said. "Even ten years too late."

A kiss with every mouthful.

She had not expected this. Of all the reactions she might have imagined in Salah, the last would have been that he would actually want to bed her. Flames burst into life in her stomach. No. No.

"Just so long as you don't expect me to keep mine," she said grimly.

He smiled. "But I know well that you do not keep your promises, Desi. Who knows better than I? That other one you promised to marry and then did not?"

The bitter memory was bile in her throat. "I changed my mind there."

"Yes," he said with emphasis. "You changed your mind."

Why was he doing this? What did he want? She was miles from understanding him. For years she had waited for his call, hoping against hope. Until her love died and nothing was left but dust and ashes. He must know that. The choice had been his.

"And you didn't, I suppose?"

He stared at her for a long, electric moment during which his eyes seemed to pierce her soul. A hard, angry gaze that was nothing like the boy she had loved. Then he tore off a bit of bread, plucked up a sprig of the greenery, wrapped it expertly in the bread, and held it out to her.

"This I told you of. *Sabzi-o-naan.* This is traditional in the mountains."

Desi took it and put it into her mouth. The pungent taste of a herb she didn't recognize exploded in her mouth and nostrils, sweet and fresh, and she made an involuntary noise of surprise.

His eyelids dropped to hide his eyes for a moment, then his dark gaze burned her. "I taught you to make that sound," he said hoarsely. "I thought it would be the music of all the rest of my life."

Heat rushed through her at his words, tearing at defences she now saw were pitifully weak. "Stop this," she said.

He reached for the herbs again, pulling off a sprig that he put into his own mouth.

"Stop?" he handed her another little bouquet of *naan-*

wrapped herb. "How, stop? You are here in my country, where you promised to come. Now I keep my side of the bargain. I promised you would delight in these herbs. Do you?"

She took it from him again, and put it in her mouth, because there was nothing else to do. Not even in her nightmares had she imagined such ferocity as this.

"Very nice," she said woodenly.

"The freshness in your mouth. I told you then that I would kiss you after every bite." Her lips parted in a little gasp. "A kiss with every mouthful. You remember, Desi? Shall I keep that part of the promise, even though ten years have passed?"

"No, I don't," she said woodenly, and "No," again.

"No?" he said. She couldn't see his eyes. "That is not what you came for, my kiss? But then, what did you come here for, Desi? Why do you come to my country, to the heart of my family, if not for this?"

He offered her another little twist of bread and herb, but she shook her head and reached into the basket herself.

"Why did you get involved?" she countered. "There was no need!"

"But yes!" he lifted a palm. "My father was determined to allow you to visit. The rest followed."

"He said he would arrange a guide. Why should it be you?"

"Who else? You know what I owe your family—so many years of hospitality! You know that such hospitality must be reciprocated." A fleeting instinct told her there was something else here, but she was too bombarded to be able to pin it down. "So, Desi, I say to you that you knew your guide would be me. Our meeting was inevitable. And I ask again, why are you here? What do you want from me?"

"I want nothing from you, Salah." She opened her mouth to tell him that she would hire someone else to be her guide, thought of Sami, and closed it again. He was right, after all.

This was all according to plan. He was only mistaken in whose plan it was.

"Why do you lie? What you come for is no shame. A woman has a right to experience pleasure. If her Western lover can't give it to her, she must look for one who does."

"I'm sure you're right," she countered. "But believe me when I say I really don't need to search so far afield."

He lifted his hands. "How can I believe it, when you are here?"

A puff of irritated laughter escaped her.

"And even if I did, you are the very last person I'd come to."

"No," he said, with such certainty she almost believed he could read her mind.

"Trust me, Salah," she said. "You are imagining this. Every part of what you imagine is the product of your own fantasy. I am not remotely interested in reviving old times with you."

He laughed and before she could stop him, clasped her wrist. She felt her pulse hammering against his thumb. She thought he was going to pull her against him again, it would be so easy, but abruptly he let go.

"It is in your blood. In every part of you. As in me," he said, with a kind of angry self-contempt. Her heart kicked.

He waved a sultan's wave and a waiter came from nowhere and cleared the little baskets away.

Now there was nothing but space between them. He lay resting on one elbow, looking at her. He didn't move, but he seemed to come closer. Drawing back was agonizing to her, an iron filing trying to move out of the magnet's powerful field.

"Shall we make love here, Desi, as we did under the dock?"

"Don't be—"

"I can tell them to go. We will blow out the candles. There will be only you and me and the stars."

"And your conscience." She felt desperate, grasping at anything that would keep him away. "Wouldn't that get in the way?"

"My conscience?"

"Aren't you engaged to Sami?" she said.

Seven

She hadn't meant to blurt that out. She had planned to act as if she didn't know. Some things she could do. Pretend to be someone who would go after her best friend's fiancé wasn't one of them.

But Desi was grasping at any defence. It had become sharply clear in the past few minutes that she could not trust herself if Salah made a serious assault. The armour that had served her for years was not up to this challenge. Her heart was melting with grief and regret, her skin was electric with feeling.

She wouldn't let it happen. It would be a betrayal of everything. It would kill her to make love with him.

"But isn't that why you've come just at this moment, Desi?"

"What do you mean?"

"Your timing is too good to be coincidence. You know I can never again make love to you once I am married. Our chance would be lost forever."

"You don't think being engaged to my best friend puts you out of bounds already?"

"We are not engaged. No discussions have yet taken place. And a man must come to terms with his past before he marries, isn't that so?" Salah said. "So that he can go to his wife without…regret. You have haunted me, Desi, how can you imagine otherwise? If I am going to marry, first I should have—what do you call it?—closure."

Her heart was beating in hard, painful thumps. In her worst imaginings she had not foreseen losing control over the proceedings so quickly.

"And how, exactly, would sex with me give you closure?" she asked bitterly. "Is it an ego thing? Are you hoping to hear me say that sex with you set the benchmark and nothing since has lived up to it?"

"Is it true?"

"No, it is not!"

"You always lied badly," he said.

"And you always had an ego as thick as butter."

"I judge by my own experience, Desi," he said.

The admission rushed through her like wildfire. She felt faint.

"I don't believe you! A few weeks, ten years ago!"

"And what about you? Don't you, too, wish for this closure?"

"I got closure long ago," she lied. No closure was possible for a blow like the one he'd delivered. "The day you told me I was soiled merchandise."

"And this old man, was he a good lover?" Salah asked, an expression in his eyes she couldn't read.

"What old man would that be?"

"The one you nearly married, Desi. Do you forget lovers so easily? Did he please you as I did?"

"Leo was forty-five!"

"Was it—"

"And it's none of your bloody business!"

She picked up one of the glasses and took a gulp of water. It blasted into her mouth, burned her throat, stung her nerves. She gasped and coughed.

"My God! What *is* this?" she cried, staring down at the glass in horror.

Salah laughed aloud. "Wine, Desi," he said, just as her brain belatedly interpreted the taste and gave her the answer.

"Oh, that's wild!" The tension of the past minutes exploded into laughter as she sank back against the cushions. "For a minute there I thought you…" she broke off when she saw where she was heading. "Have you ever done that?"

"Tried to poison you?"

"Drunk one thing when you were expecting something else!"

"In England, once," he confided, "I drank what I thought was coffee. It was not coffee. For two seconds, I thought, *they have given me pigs' urine to insult me!* Then I realized it was tea."

She let out a whoop. The incident shook them both out of the mood of angry recrimination. They lay laughing together over nothing, like the old days, the old nights, under the moonlit dock.

They had always laughed together. It was one of the things she'd loved most, missed most…

Laughter shared with a lover. It didn't get better than that.

And now, when he was no longer threatening, when her guard was down, the layers of protection she had laid down over the past tore away. In one moment she was naked again. Her heart coiled with yearning. Oh, what had they done? What had they lost?

The waiter arrived with the next course, a tray with a dozen little dishes that all looked impossibly succulent. Just as Salah had promised, ten years ago.

She had to stop this. Salah was already dangerous enough without help from her own feelings. If there was one thing she was not going to do on this trip, it was get seduced into sex for the sake of closure.

For him it would be closure. For her, she saw suddenly, it might be just the opposite.

Desi sat up and tucked her feet under her.

"So, when do we go?" she asked in a bright voice, as the dishes, one by one, were laid on the cloth between them. "Do we leave first thing in the morning?"

He jerked his chin in the way she remembered. "Not tomorrow. You need at least a day to acclimatize before going into the desert. Maybe two."

"But—"

"And I have business tomorrow. The day after, if you insist. At sunrise."

She nodded agreement. "How long does it take to get to the site?"

"How long?" Salah was examining the various offerings with close attention. "That depends."

"It *depends?* On what?"

The last dish was set down, the waiter bowed and left, and Salah began spooning various bits of food onto a small plate.

"On what?" he repeated absently. "Oh—it may depend on the weather, the wind…"

"The *wind?* What, we'll be sailing?" she asked ironically.

"You are not so ignorant about the desert that you do not know that wind can be a dangerous enemy."

"I suppose weathermen predict the weather in Barakat as well as elsewhere."

"Climate change impacts the desert as well as elsewhere, also."

"So a big wind might blow up from nowhere and we'll get stuck in the sand?"

"It is not unknown. Not even unusual. Try this, Desi," Salah said, reaching out a long arm to set an array of taster-size morsels in front of her.

The odour of the food reached her nostrils then, utterly intoxicating.

"Oh, that smells amazing!" she cried, scooping up a morsel of something mysterious, then heaved a sigh as the flavour hit her taste buds. "That's delicious. That's the food of the gods!"

You make it sound like the food of the gods, she had said.

He looked at her, and she knew he was there again, too. She sought for something to say to dislodge the time shift.

"So do we—"

"Why does my father's work interest you, Desi?"

Her heart sank. She tossed her hair back to look at him. "It was all in my letter. Didn't your father tell you?"

"You tell me."

Damn. This wasn't fair. The letter, mostly composed by Sami, was supposed to have paved the way, established all the lies. Desi was all right about *living* the lie, since so much depended on it, but she hated having to *tell* it, face to face. Especially to Salah. Especially now.

Especially as it was, she knew, so ludicrously unlikely a lie.

"Did he tell you that I'm going back to university to do a degree?"

"Now?"

She nodded uncomfortably. "I'll start part-time this year…if I can. Middle Eastern history and archaeology."

"Why? Don't you have a very successful career?"

"Modelling won't last forever," she said, and it was perfectly true. "I want a smooth transition when the time comes."

"A smooth transition into archaeology? What awoke this sudden interest?"

"Not that sudden. I've been curious about archaeology ever since that summer the university came to dig on the island," she said. "Remember that First Nations site they were digging? We used to go and watch every day. I never forgot the thrill of seeing someone uncover an arrowhead!"

That part at least was true: eleven-year-old Desi had been fascinated as the past was unveiled: the discovery of the floor of the longhouse, the settlement's refuse mound, the arrowheads of chipped stone. One of the students had encouraged her interest, telling her what each find said about the people who had lived on the site, showing her how the history of two hundred years ago could be discovered even without written records.

"Two hundred years?" Salah had said in youthful disdain. "In my country we have cities five thousand years old!"

Desi had reacted to the challenge with predictable outrage. "So what?" she had cried. "I bet there are lots of countries where they have them *ten* thousand years old!"

His mouth smiled when she reminded him; his eyes were too shadowed to read.

"You made me so mad! But I think I made up my mind then that one day I'd come to Barakat and see what you were talking about, a city five thousand years old!"

"And now you are here."

She hated the way he said it.

"Won't you find archaeology tame after a career as a supermodel?"

"It beats marketing a perfume called *Desirée*," she said dryly. Her distaste for that at least was no lie. "'*Feminine, delicate, but with a smouldering hint of sensuality.'* Or a chain of restaurants: *Desi's Diner.* How would *you* like it?"

He had the grace to laugh.

"But isn't a chain of restaurants with a smouldering hint of sensuality just what the world needs?"

She rolled her eyes. "Not from me."

"And only an urgent visit to my father's site will save you from this fate?"

How she hated the lies! But Sami's anguished voice was there in her head… *I've only got one chance to derail this thing…*

"I told you—it's the only time I have free," she said. "This is the time I go to the island every year. I thought how great if I could get in on the ground floor with your father and he let me volunteer on the site for a couple of seasons. That's a requirement of the course."

The explanation had sounded halfway reasonable during the planning stage. She wasn't sure now.

To her relief, Salah hardly seemed to hear. He was tearing at a chicken wing.

"Try this," he said, leaning right over to hold up to her mouth a piece thick with a purply-black sauce. Desi automatically opened her mouth and bit into the tender flesh, then grunted at the rich, melting flavour.

"Mmm! What *is* that black stuff? I've never tasted anything so yummy in my life!" she said when she could speak.

"Pomegranate sauce. Another speciality of the mountain tribes."

A drop of sauce was on her cheek too far for her tongue to reach. Salah caught it with a fingertip and presented it to her mouth. She licked instinctively, then her eyes flew to his.

He slid his wet finger deliberately across her lower lip.

The hoarse intake of her breath told him everything. A jolt

of electricity zapped the night air. In his black eyes two tiny golden flames were reflected, as if to warn her his touch would burn. His white teeth tore off a bite from the same piece he had offered her, and the sensual intimacy of that hit her another blow.

Desi dropped her eyes and made a business of wiping her cheek with a napkin. She tried to think of something to say, but her mind had been tipped onto its back and lay there, kicking helplessly. She felt gauche, inexperienced. As if the ten years were smoke and mirrors.

Silence fell, a silence thick with feeling, expectation, a question asked and answered.

She began to eat.

The little lamps on the cloth lighted his hand as he ate, emphasizing the strength of his fingers, the fluid grace of his wrist that transformed into power whenever he grasped a bit of *naan* or a goblet. Involuntarily the memory came to her of that same hand, painted in moonlight and shadow, rough and tender with inexperienced passion as they lay under the dock.

Sometimes, too, his mouth and jaw were touched with gold: a stern mouth, a full lower lip that the chiaroscuro painted in more sensual lines than was revealed in ordinary light. His eyes were mostly shadowed, except for a black glinting in the darkness.

"You go to the island still?" he asked. She wished he had started any topic but that one, but she had to answer.

"My parents live there full time now. I spend a month there every summer, and Christmas if I can."

He asked after her parents, her young sister, after Harry, her brother. Softly, softly, he drew her into remembering. She knew it was deliberate, to prove some point, to set some mood—but she could neither prevent it, nor resist.

The shadows, the stars, his voice, the talk of those island

summers—everything conspired to take her back to the sweet hours they had lain undetected and undisturbed in their refuge under the ancient dock, their world of two. She began to feel like that child-woman again, on the brink of discovery of self and other, of love and desire, of her own sexual power, and another's.

He had been her lover. She knew what it meant for those hands, with light and shadow playing on them like this, to caress and stroke her. Sometimes when his hand disappeared again into shadow, her body shivered in the unconscious expectation of a caress.

Desi sank into the embracing cushions as they talked, her legs folded with unconscious grace, naked toes curling as she rested on one elbow and ate with her fingers. All her guard had come down. She was eating more food than she'd had at one go for a decade. This was a total sensual delight.

He watched her soften, and the predator in him gloried in his success even as he told himself it meant nothing.

The last course was put in front of them then, a pastry oozing with the promise of sweetness, and she summoned resistance at last. "That looks lovely, but I never eat sugar," she said.

"This is made with honey."

"Or honey." But for once she could not resist. "Just a taste," Desi said.

Fatal mistake. "Oh, that is just too delicious!" she exclaimed, hastily dropping the little gold fork.

Salah bent his head, and she saw his eyes clearly. They glinted amusement at her, and something else, and her blood leapt so painfully in response she almost whimpered.

"Do you push temptation away so easily, *Deezee?*" he asked, his voice caressing her nerve endings like soft sandpaper.

She looked at him, a hard man if there ever was one. "Don't you?"

"Not such temptation as this," he said. She knew he did not mean the little honey-crusted sweet. Flame flickering in the black eyes, he picked up the sweetmeat from her plate with his fingers, tilted his head back and caught it on his tongue.

It nearly flattened her. Sensation roared over her skin, bringing every cell to attention.

His gaze caught hers before she could turn away, and it was all there in her eyes. She saw him read it. The heat rose up in her cheeks, but she could not tear her gaze from his.

Her eyes were emerald with desire. He smiled like a wolf, dark and determined, and said what he did not want to say....

"Shall I come to your bed tonight, Desi?"

Warmth flooded her body. Oh, how could she be so weak? She'd had ten years to get over this!

"No."

He shrugged. "Then you must come to mine."

"Mmm. I'll be riding a flying pig."

She was falling apart, and it was only the first day. Desi took a deep, trembling breath. She was headed out of her depth here. The sooner she got out of the palace and onto the dig with other people, the better.

She sat up, drew her legs under her, pressed a cushion behind her back.

"So, you never actually told me: how many hours will we be on the road?"

"Hours? What do you mean?"

"What do *you* mean?"

"Desi, the trip across the desert will take four days at least, probably five."

Eight

How was flight? Have you seen HIM yet?

Where R U?? Please call!

There were five texts from Sami on her BlackBerry, each one more frantic than the last, and a half a dozen missed calls. Desi should have texted Sami from the Arrivals hall or, failing that, the car, and was stunned to realize she had forgotten. She'd completely forgotten her phone, if not her life, from the moment she'd met Salah.

Has he murdered U? What is going onnnnnnnnn?

Desi sat with the thing in her hand. She should call Sami to update her, but…she just did not want to talk about Salah and their meeting and the dinner she'd just shared with him.

Or the fact that she had turned down the chance to share his bed.

Meanwhile, she had to respond.

Sry, sry!! Horrible jetlag. S picked me up, going to sleep now. Ttyl, she sent.

She ruthlessly shut the phone off before Sami could call. Then she lay in the fairytale bed, surrounded by soft lamp-light and ancient luxury, trying to think. Trying to get distance on the evening she had just experienced.

Five days in the desert alone with Salah! How was it possible? How had Sami not known?

What would she do, alone with him day after day, night after night, a forbidding stranger who somehow shared a past with her? A man who thought making love with her would give him closure?

He wanted her. His love might be dead—he said it was, and she believed him—but Salah wanted her. She was alone now because she had chosen it. He would have come to her bed if she'd wavered for one second. If she'd flicked an eyelash.

Might he still come? She couldn't be sure. She had said no, but—he might think that if he came to her room she wouldn't be able to keep on saying it.

And he'd be right. Desi was afraid. All the defences she thought she'd built up over ten years had disappeared in the space of one short breath. She was vulnerable in a way she hadn't been with any other man. And she didn't know what he really wanted.

Closure. That was such an extraordinary thing for a man like Salah to say! What closure would sex give him? *You have haunted me, Desi.* Was it true? Or did he have some ulterior motive for saying it?

Desi flung the sheet back, swung her legs over the edge of the bed, and sat with her head in her hands. After a moment she got up and began to pace.

The intimacy of the roof garden. The constant harking on the past. The fact he had ordered food he had lovingly de-scribed to her ten years ago. The irresistible way he'd chosen tidbits for her, fed her. Painful reminders of their love, scorching tokens of intimacy, the actions of a man determined to win back an old love.

All false. All stage dressing. Salah did not want to win her back. He had made that very plain, a long time ago.

Why, then?

He wants revenge. The thought dropped into her head with an almost audible click. Four days. Five. He could find a dozen ways to get revenge, she was sure, alone with her in the desert for five days. But what could he want revenge *for?*

Everything that happened had been his own doing.

A few days after he left, Salah had phoned her. He begged her, he pleaded his love. He knew now that it was jealousy that had motivated him. He had believed that look in her eyes was only for him, and there it was in the photo, for anyone who looked at her. He had taken refuge in blaming her, too easy to do.

"But I will never do anything like that again, Desi. I will understand myself better." If only she would forgive him.

The call came too late. Their argument had shaken Desi to the core, and suddenly all the changes that before had seemed so easy frightened her. Move away from her family and friends, to a country on the other side of the world whose language she didn't speak, whose people and culture and religion she knew nothing of, where she knew no one save Salah? Have children who would be citizens of another country?

History was against them, too. That week there had been a graphic television documentary showing a woman stoned to death in the capital of Kaljukistan. Television news was full of the atrocities towards women there. Women dying because no male doctor was allowed to attend them. Girls' schools closed, women teachers and doctors thrown out of work.

Women beaten in the street by armed policemen for showing a lock of hair.

Desi was deeply frightened. How well did she really know Salah? How could she love him when she didn't know who he was?

She was too young by far to handle the terrible, contradictory feelings that raged through her at the sound of his voice.

"I don't love you," she cried.

"You do," he insisted, but he was young, too. "You love me, Desi. We love each other. I love you! I love you more than the world. Please, please, Desi, we are going to get married!"

But her wild fears had proved stronger than his young courage.

"You're just like the Kaljuks!" she accused him at last. "You want to stop me doing anything except stay at home and have babies!"

Two weeks later she learned from Sami that Salah was in Parvan, fighting alongside Prince Omar and the Cup Companions. The agonizing pain in her heart told Desi the truth of her own feelings, but there was no way to tell Salah now.

Desi had felt utterly helpless. She had destroyed something precious, and now that she saw her mistake, there was no way back.

Before she could think what to do, Leonard J. Patrick came to town.

Leonard J. Patrick was *the* hot North American modelling agent. He had a nose for what he called raw star quality. When he came gunning for Desi, her future was practically guaranteed: supermodel status, celebrity, stardom. And just then, it seemed like the answer.

He swept Desi off to the best consultants on the continent, gave her a movement coach and a personal trainer. He created a signature look for her.

Desirée. Leo launched her with fanfare, and his nose wasn't mistaken.

Sometimes she had the feeling, almost too deep to reach, that just because others envied her didn't mean the life was right for her. She ached for Salah with a need so deep it burned her.

Salah's been wounded.

Standing by an ocean, plugging one ear against the music and laughter floating from the balcony above the exclusive stretch of beach, Desi had stumbled and almost fallen, as if the ricochet from the bullet had hit her.

"Wounded? How?"

"He was leading the charge on a Kaljuk position," Sami sobbed out. "Baba's trying to find out more. We think he's in a field hospital…."

"A friend of mine has been wounded in the Parvan-Kaljuk War," Desi told Leo. "I have to go there. Please don't take any more bookings for me right now."

But hard as he tried, Leo never managed to make space in her booking calendar….

"He's back in Central Barakat," Sami told her, sobbing with a mixture of relief and grief. "He's in the best hospital, Uncle Khaled says. Oh, God, Desi, it's his *head!*"

Desi sent a card, a cute one with a patched up teddy bear. Too shy to say all that was in her heart, she wrote only a few lines. If he answered, *when* he answered, she would be braver. She knew he would answer.

If he could….

At night she dreamed of him. She dreamed he was lost somewhere in the darkness, needing her, calling her name. But she couldn't find him, and when she opened her mouth to call, she had no voice.

"He's out of danger," Sami reported, after three nightmare

weeks. "They've taken him home, my aunt is nursing him there now."

At last a letter came with a Barakati stamp. She knew, she knew it could only be from Salah, and she knew, too, that now she would have the courage to face Leo and tell him what she must: her life here was over. This was not the life for her. She belonged with Salah.

She tore it open in all innocence, her heart wide open.

It was short. Her eyes ran over the few lines, grief clawing at her even before she took in the meaning. *Why do you write me? What can we be to each other now? You betrayed your honour. A man must marry a woman of honour, or regret his foolishness all the rest of his life.*

Nine

The moonlight coming through the fan of coloured glass over the door threw shadows of red, blue and green onto her face as Desi pulled open the door and stepped out onto the balcony. All was still. Moonlight bathed the courtyard, was reflected from the smooth surface of the pool below, bright against the black water, shimmering a little as wind dusted across its surface. The tree rustled, touched by the same soft wind.

A sleepy bird asked the time. A night insect clicked and buzzed in the tumbled greenery.

The wind pressed the silk of her nightshirt against her body, the moon outlining in white gold everything the wind revealed. Wind and Moon conspiring in the revelation of beauty.

No wonder the pagans worshipped them, he thought. *When they grant such favours as this.*

She shivered, as if sensing his presence, but did not turn to the shadows where he stood waiting.

He had known she would come. True desire would always draw the desired. *Desirée*. The nightingale sang for the rose…the rose gave up her perfume to the night.

The moon rode fat and heavy in the sky, a few days to the full. Desi leaned on the parapet and looked up to where the dome glowed purple. The palace looked so different in moonlight. Mysterious, its beauty shadowed.

She had loved him so much. She had forgotten just how much. Made herself forget. But he had not killed her love. No, her love had survived that brutality. She had had to kill it by her own hand. Deliberately, so as to be able to live. It was the only way she knew to survive.

Or believed she had killed it. Tonight she understood that her love was a river driven underground, but no less a raging torrent for being secret. Now it flooded up from the fertile earth of her being, smashing its way into the light, gaining strength from the years of being suppressed.

Hot tears stung her eyes. "Salah," she whispered. "Oh, Salah."

And in that breath he was there, hard and real, his strong arms wrapping her in a sudden, fierce embrace against his naked chest.

"I knew you would come," he growled, and even as she protested, his lips came down hard and possessive on hers. He kissed her until her protest was a moan of deliverance, until the hand that pressed against him melted into submission against his chest, moved up around his neck. Then he swept her up in his arms and carried her back through the doorway to the tumbled bed.

He laid her down among the tossed sheets, but did not take his mouth from hers for a moment. With one hand he tore off the sarong that was the only garment he wore, releasing his hot, hard flesh to press against her thigh as he flung himself against the length of her.

He was consumed with need. He was a fool, but this had been inevitable from the moment he saw her. Her power over him had only increased with time and absence, though he had believed it would be otherwise. Now memory was conspiring with her beautiful sensuality to bring him down.

But at least he would take her with him: she, too, was lost....

Never had she met such ferocity in a kiss. His lips devoured her, setting fire to her blood. He had laid her on the bed and stretched his long body beside her, and still his mouth did not let her go.

One hand caressed and held her throat, pushed at the silk collar, the heat of flesh on flesh. Then there was the high shriek of a tear, and cool air breathed over her breast, for a moment before the fire of his hand clasped her and stroked her.

Her flesh was scorched by the burning need in his touch. Her body arced under his kiss and lifted hungrily against the hungry palm enclosing her breast.

His hand slipped from her breast then, moved against her back, her stomach, her hip, discovering and defining at the same time. Then his hand moved to her thigh, and he cupped her sex with ferocious possession. She melted as if that statement of ownership alone would be enough to bring her to the peak.

He began to stroke her, his fingers hot and strong and knowing, and her body lifted wildly to the pleasure of his touch. She whimpered with pleasure and yearning, the sounds he remembered, and still he did not lift his hungry mouth, but drank in those little mews like wine.

She opened her mouth wider then, as pleasure climbed in her, and he thrust his tongue into the warm hollow, till the double assault left her sobbing with pleasure.

His mouth tore away from hers , and he lifted his head, and looked down into her face for one long, tortured moment before his mouth found hers again, plunging, hungry, devouring.

She was aflame, melted, an inferno of need. A fire of desire she hadn't known existed roared up in her, consuming thought, reason, everything except the fact that he was there and she needed him.

His body was hard and urgent against her, as if with the need of years, and her hand found and encircled the hard, seeking flesh, and his groan shivered along her nerves to send her joy a notch higher.

Still the silk of her shirt thwarted his intent. He lifted away from her, grasped the fabric in two hands and ripped it again and again until it parted for him from top to bottom.

She lay with her body exposed now in the soft lamplight, exposed to the fire of his gaze, her throat arched and inviting as she looked up at him. His eyes ran greedily over the perfection of her, painted with the golden glow—hair, eyes, mouth, breasts, waist, hips, sex, thighs, ankles…sex.

He drew her against him then, the whole length of her bare skin aligned with his, and his arms wrapped her. Her face pressed into the hollow of his shoulder as his hand curved behind and between her thighs. Gently his fingers slipped into the moist depths that waited for him.

He stroked the delicate lips while her moist breath panted against his throat in little pleasured moans. His touch was sure, as if he had known her body intimately for ten years, or as if it had been waiting for this moment all that time. In what seemed seconds she lifted against his expert touch, crying and sighing, a sound he remembered as if from yesterday.

She mewed and slid down from the peak, and then he drew away from her. Then his hand clasped her thigh, lifted her leg up, and his body shifted against her and, with a thrust that made her cry out, he pushed his way home at last.

He filled her to bursting. She cried out, arching into a pleasure that she had not experienced in ten long years. "Salah!" she cried, in a voice he remembered, and a groan was torn from his own throat.

His body thrust again and again into the hot nest of her, and with each thrust they cried out together. His hand cupped her neck, so that they looked into each other's eyes. She stroked his strong chest, his arms, greedily, hungry for the feel of his skin, and every caress drove him higher.

"How I have waited for this!" he cried then, gazing into her eyes, then down at the place where their bodies met, and his look held such passionate hunger that her pleasure began to peak in an overwhelming burst and she sobbed with too much pleasure.

It was too much for them both. The pitch of their joy, and their need, was overwhelming. He grunted, pushed in again and again, and as she melted into powerful, sobbing release, his head lifted, his neck arched up, his body swelled harder, made a convulsive thrust, and then he cried out with her, a long, involuntary sound that was half weeping, half joy, and fell down against her.

Desi awoke to shaded sunlight and lay for a moment in a mood of lazy well-being, wondering why it should be so. Behind her head the breeze blew in through the wooden slats shading the window, cool and fresh. As she yawned and stretched a muscle protested, and she remembered what had happened in the night. A smile played over her lips and she turned her head.

The bed beside her was empty. It was late, and he had said he had work today. She was not sorry. She needed time to think.

Ten years. She stretched like a cat, feeling that her arteries carried warm honey instead of blood from her heart to her body. Ten long years since she had felt this magic in her limbs.

He wants to marry Sami.

Her heart contracted at the thought, withdrawing the honey from her muscles, and Desi flung herself to her feet. What had she done? What kind of fool was she?

Sami was right. Salah had never got over her. The thought touched her in some deep part of herself that she was afraid to look at more closely.

She hadn't got over Salah, either, that much was obvious. It might have been better if she had had some suspicion that that was the case, Desi reflected. She had been totally unprepared for the onslaught of his feelings, and her own. And she had fallen at the first fence.

Closure. If Salah now felt he had closure, she had done Sami no good at all. Instead of putting up a roadblock, she had only paved his way to marriage with her friend.

And as for her—what grief had she stored up for herself?

Breakfast was served to her in her suite, where she sat on cushions at a low table, beside a window open onto the fountain. Salah, Fatima told her, had arranged for one of the chauffeurs to take her on a tour of the city if she wished.

Desi spent a restless day, wandering through mosques and gardens, around the magnificent tomb and gardens of a thirteenth century Barakati poet. It was all beautiful and impressive: soaring domes, exquisite mosaic and delicate stone arabesques, but Desi could take it in with only half her awareness. She kept thinking about what had happened last night, and what might be going to happen tonight.

Was once enough to give Salah the closure he was looking

for? How could she bear to be with him for so many days and nights, with this bottomless need assailing her, if he no longer wanted her?

Another bout of the heartbreak she'd suffered ten years ago would kill her.

In the late afternoon, as she got into the car after a visit to a small, breathtakingly ancient mosque, her phone beeped with a text. Sami, just waking up in Vancouver.

How RU? What's happening? Talk to me!

OK. Nothing to report, lied Desi, who just could not talk about what had happened. *Sightseeing in city today, with guide. Leaving 2morrow 4 site.*

Who is guide? Sami wanted to know.

Today, Faraj. Tomorrow, Salah. TRIP TAKES 5 DAYS ACROSS DESERT!!! WHY DIDN'T YOU WARN ME?

OMG! I had no idea. Vry sry but at least will give u lots of time to work your magic! Car will be air conditioned, LOL.

It's not the heat, it's the COMPANY!

ROFLMAO. Good luck. U know I wish u every success...

That was, oddly enough, the first time it occurred to her that if, for reasons of his own, Salah really was set on marrying Sami, he would not be very happy if she, Desi, managed to sabotage his plans. If she succeeded in getting permission for Sami to marry Farid from Khaled al Khouri against Salah's wishes, five days in his company on the way to the site would be nothing compared to five days in his company on the return....

She could only cross that bridge when she came to it.

She arrived back at the palace at the end of the day sunburnt, tired and hungry, and desperate to see Salah again. Desperate to know that something had been awakened in him by their lovemaking.

"His Excellency not come. All meeting very hard all,"

Fatima said. "He say tomorrow come up at *fajr*, breakfast very quick. You live after *fajr*. In summer go early!"

"Get up at *fajr?*"

Fatima shook her head with her inability to translate the word. Thinking it must be a number, Desi held up fingers. "Seven o'clock? Six? Eight?"

Fatima, too, began to use sign language. She looked up and moved her hands in a broad arc. "Sky night, not sun. Sun—" she stretched one arm out to indicate the horizon and wiggled her fingers.

"Sunrise? Get up with the sun?"

Fatima shook her head vigorously. "Before sun! *Fajr. Muezzin!*"

Muezzin, she remembered, meant the call to prayer. The first call to prayer came when the world was still dark. So they would set out before daybreak.

That entailed no particular hardship for Desi, who might not wake up for less than ten thousand dollars, but who, when she did so, was often required in Makeup while the sky was still black.

But it was difficult to wait so long to see Salah. The more so as she suspected he was deliberately avoiding her. She would like to know why. Because he feared his own reactions, feared to be tempted again? Because he was feeling guilty about what had happened?

Or, worst—because once was enough, and now he would find it a burden to be with her?

Desi felt confused, at odds with herself. What did it mean, that she still wanted Salah, in spite of everything? That the sexual bond was as powerful now—more powerful, perhaps, with maturity—after ten years of thinking she hated him?

Why had she come here, and stirred up this hornet's nest?

She ate alone, listening as the evening *muezzin* made his

call, turned down Fatima's invitation to watch television, and went to bed early. She was still jetlagged, and dawn would come early.

She phoned Sami, and was relieved when she got her friend's voicemail.

"It's me. We're leaving tomorrow at first light, and apparently there's no coverage in the desert without a satellite phone," Desi said. "So I'll be incommunicado for a few days. I know you wish me luck."

She was restless. She read for a little, then knelt up on the bed, turned out the lamp, opened the wooden jalousie, and rested her elbows on the window sill, gazing out on the silent courtyard and the stars.

If only she could get a sense of where she was headed! But the future was as black and impenetrable as the sky. She felt nothing—no sense of impending doom anymore, no promise of release. Only an intense, unbearable yearning for his presence. His arms, his mouth, his body. *Please, please, let him come to me…*

After awhile she slipped down into bed. She didn't notice when sleep came.

She woke suddenly. Through the open window above her bed she saw stars in a clear black sky. A cooling breeze blew in over her, shaking the wooden jalousie, but that sound was not what had awakened her.

She leaned up and put her hand out to the lamp. Before she could turn it on, he was there, kneeling beside the bed.

"Desi." His voice was hoarse with the struggle against longing. *"Deezee."*

She reached for him, and in the next moment his body was hot against hers and she was drowning.

Ten

The sun flamed up in the sky on the right, a perfect circle of burning fury that promised the greater ferocity to come, and the grey line of the mountains' shadow rushed towards them, chased by golden sand.

"That's quite a vista," Desi murmured. It was a dizzying view all the way to white-topped Mount Shir, brooding high above the foothills like the lion it was named for.

Salah glanced at her, and away again. She looked like what she was—a beautiful woman who had known passion in the night. And he realized, from the change he saw in her, that it had been a long time since she had experienced the kind of lovemaking he had given her. Her skin had a glow that had not been there before; her eyes were soft with remembered pleasure, her mouth was swollen with the memory of kisses.

His kisses.

He felt a burst of masculine satisfaction. That was the

measure of a man, or one of them: to give his woman true pleasure—so that afterwards she was sweet, like honey. His own body ached and sang with the thought of her sweetness, and for him, too, it had been lovemaking like nothing he had known for ten years.

"I told you once that you would like it," he said, but he was not talking about Mount Shir.

Then he heard his own thoughts—*his woman.* But she was not his woman, not now, not ever again. And he was a fool if he let sex cloud his thinking about her. She had betrayed him once, when he needed her most. She was almost certainly betraying him now, betraying his country, perhaps—for although he had no proof of what he really wanted here, he could be very sure at least that she was lying to him.

Sex made fools of men. He knew that, he had seen it happen to others. He would not be of their number. He would keep a clear head. He had four or five days to get the truth from her. Desire must not blind him to the need to do it. Sex must not be allowed to interfere with his plans. He reached out and pressed the radio into life, to puncture the mood in the truck's cabin.

He had been ten times a fool to think he could undertake this task without risk.

Desi smiled and stretched in her seat, letting the incomprehensible chatter from the radio blend into the background like music. Every muscle in her body simultaneously protested and relayed a honeyed memory of the lovemaking just past.

Salah had been wild with need in the night, seeking the solace of her body over and over, as if to make up for ten lost years in a single night. When they arose at daybreak Desi had no idea whether she'd slept. The mix of languor and energy in her body was like nothing she'd ever experienced before.

The memory of their lovemaking was in the vehicle with them now, heavy in the air, liquid in her cells. She was sensitive even to the pressure of the air against her skin; any movement was slow dancing in honey.

A few more minutes of driving in shade, and then, with a little explosion of light, they were in full sunshine.

There was a smile in her being, and it played with her eyes and the corners of her mouth. Desi leaned lazily back and watched the landscape. Silence fell for minutes, during which she savoured shimmering crystal sharp air, blinding light, purple-grey shadows under distant foothills.

Watching the shadows retreat across the desert as the sun climbed higher could almost be a life's occupation, she reflected. And again she had that strange feeling of belonging, as if the desert had been waiting for her and would now claim her.

He had not mentioned the letter, but she thought he would soon. He had to. Could he explain, would he apologize? Surely now they could discuss what had happened so long ago with some detachment?

She shifted nervously. Everything was too overwhelming, happening too fast. If he did bring it up, where would that lead them? Was she ready for that?

Would she end up telling him about Sami, she wondered suddenly? No real explanation was possible between them without that, but…how would he react? She had promised Sami she would not tell Salah. If she risked betraying that…she had no idea where the discussion would go.

"So much traffic!" she said. "Does everybody start early, or have they been driving all night?"

"This is the main road to the oil fields. In summer everyone avoids driving in the middle of the day."

In his voice she thought she heard a reflection of her own nervous reluctance to start on something where they could not be sure of the end. Well, there was time. Five days they would be alone. Five days to try to sort her thoughts. No hurry.

They drove in silence. Now and then Salah pointed out an ancient ruin in the desert, or a distant nomad encampment. Desi laughed aloud when they came up behind a pickup truck carrying a young camel which was hunkered down with its legs folded beneath it, complacently regarding them over the tailgate, chewing its cud.

"And my camera's packed in my case!"

"You have a camera?"

"Of course! I want to—"

"You will not be able to take photographs at the dig," Salah said.

"Oh! Is—" But she was afraid to ask why for fear of exposing her ignorance. "Have you been to the dig before?" she asked instead.

"A few times," Salah said. "When it was first discovered."

"What can you tell me about it? I couldn't find any information. Sami said it might be contemporary with Sumer. It sounds really exciting."

It was barely three weeks since Desi had first heard of Sumer, the ancient civilisation that thrived between the Tigris and Euphrates Rivers five thousand years ago, but she wasn't faking her interest. There was something about five thousand years of history that sparked her imagination now as much as when she was eleven.

She had crammed a lot of study into the short time she had to prepare. But although she could bone up on the Sumer period and archaeology in general, she had found absolutely nothing about the site Salah's father was working, so far from where ancient Sumer had prospered. Some mysterious outpost, some far city?

"My father is maintaining very close secrecy until he can

publish," he said. "You he could not refuse, but no other outsider has been allowed to visit. No media. A hand-picked team. You understand."

"I see," Desi said lamely, who didn't know what it meant to "publish" a site, couldn't imagine why an ancient site would be kept secret, and was dismayed to learn she was on the receiving end of such a massive favour. "I didn't realize what I was asking for. I mean…"

"Are you sure?"

"Sure?"

"Sure you didn't realize what you were asking for."

His voice was hard suddenly. In anyone else she would have called it suspicious, but what could he be suspicious of as far as the dig went?

"I'm new at this," she pointed out mildly.

"And just by chance you happen upon the most tightly kept secret of archaeology of the last thirty years and discover an interest."

It *was* suspicion. She couldn't imagine what he suspected her of, but after last night, how could he speak to her in such a voice?

"I didn't go looking for this, you know," she pointed out calmly. "Sami is my best friend. Why shouldn't she tell me about her uncle's work when I told her what I was planning? I'm sure she has no idea how secret it is. She'd have said something."

"Sami should not know about it herself."

"She knows because it's the reason marriage negotiations aren't taking place yet. Till your father gets back from the dig. But by all means let's not discuss the dig if you'd rather not!" Desi said. "Let's talk about something else. We've made love two nights running. Have you got the closure you wanted?"

Immediately she wished the words unsaid.

Salah turned his head and looked at her with a look so smouldering she felt physical heat. Memory roared up, making her weak.

"Have you?" he countered.

"I wasn't the one looking for closure. Why won't you give me a straight answer?"

"You were looking for something. Have you got it yet?"

"I was looking to go to your father's dig," she snapped. How much hurt he could still inflict! "Are we there yet? No? Well, then, not."

He flicked a glance into her eyes.

"So you didn't come here to see me?"

"Salah, how many times do you need that question answered?"

"Truthfully, only once."

"By which you mean, you won't accept any answer till you hear what you want to hear. I'm happy to oblige. What answer would you like? Let's get it out of the way."

"Desi." His voice was almost pleading, and her eyes jerked involuntarily to his face. "I know that you are not here for the reason you say. I know you. You can't tell me a lie and I don't know it."

"You don't know anything about me," she said, as bitterness welled up in her throat. "You don't know me now, you didn't know me then. You couldn't have written that letter if you'd known the first thing about me."

He shook his head at the attempt to derail him. "Tell me why you have come."

"Not from any motive you are contemplating."

"Is that an admission? What motive, then?"

"Oh, leave it alone!"

The honeyed languour was gone from her body. Sunlight was beating into the car with such ferocity she was getting a headache. Heat and sun rarely bothered her, she blossomed in the heat, but this was different. A strip of chrome on the wing mirror was reflecting the sun straight into her eyes. She realized she hadn't put on her sunglasses, opened her bag and pulled them out.

"Hiding your eyes won't help."

"On the contrary, it may prevent a headache," she said sharply. A herd of camels grazed on nothing in front of a settlement of half a dozen mudbrick houses. Tourists pressed cameras against the windows of a bus, snapping pictures as they passed. The highway curved around to the west; Mount Shir was behind them now. Ahead was an endless stretch of sand, shimmering in the heat, the highway a silver-grey ribbon laid across the vastness.

The road to nowhere, she thought.

After lunch in a small village restaurant, where they waited out the midday heat for another hour, Salah turned the four wheel drive vehicle off-road and struck out across the dunes.

Now they were completely alone. Within a few minutes they had left all signs of civilisation behind, and were surrounded by the rich emptiness of the desert. Heat shimmered over the dunes; the sun was a white blast furnace against a blue of startling intensity; the pale sand, broken by rocky outcrops now and then, stretched to infinity. Only when she turned to look back at Mount Shir was there any relief for her eyes.

After several hours, the sun began to set ahead of them, the sky turning fiery red and orange and the sun getting fatter and heavier as it approached the horizon. As she watched, the sky shaded to purple, and now the sun was a massive orange ball, larger than she recalled ever seeing it before. When it began to sink behind the horizon, the sky above turned midnight blue.

The sun disappeared in a blaze; the sky went black very quickly. And still they drove.

Salah did not put on the headlights. The world was shadows. There was no human light visible anywhere, just stars and a moon almost at the full, bathing the dunes in ghostly purple. Desi was seized with a sudden, atavistic dread.

She shifted nervously. "When do we stop for the night?"

"Soon," he said. "An hour or so. Are you tired?"

She shrugged and took a sip of water from the bottle ever present between them.

"A little. Aren't you going to put the headlights on?"

"What for?"

"Can you drive in the dark?"

"Why not?"

"But how do you know where you're going?"

Salah laughed. "There is only one way to navigate in the desert, Desi—by the sky. In daylight, by the sun. At night, by the stars. My forebears have done it for many thousands of years. Don't worry—if my ancestors had not been good navigators, I would not be here."

She laughed, and the strange dread lifted. They spoke little, but a feeling of peace and companionship settled over her as they drove on into the night. She almost forgot the harsh accusations of the morning in her pleasure at being with Salah in a world of two.

She had no idea how long they drove when at last a flickering light appeared in the distance. "What's that? Is that a town?"

"You will see," he said, and flicked on the headlights.

A cluster of strangely patterned tents met her eyes: a Bedouin encampment. By the time they reached it, a party of tall robed men was there to welcome them. Under instruction, Salah parked the Toyota against the wire fence of an enclosure, and they got out to be greeted by the men.

They were a tall race, clearly. The men towered over her in their flowing robes and turbans, with the dignified bearing of those who have never lost their connection to the land. They chatted with Salah in soft welcoming voices and led them past the wire enclosure, which proved to be a camel corral. In the flickering torchlight as they passed she saw a dozen beasts crouching on the ground, chewing and whuffling, their outrageous long curling eyelashes made even more seductive by moonshadow. Her heart leapt with the alien magic.

They were led to the centre of the encampment of tents, where there was torchlight and a charcoal brazier. Other men were moving about, laying a carpet with plates and food. Another took their bags and disappeared.

"Is this a hotel?" Desi asked in amazement.

"It is a nomad camp. But the people are by tradition very hospitable. They are used to strangers appearing out of the desert. There are guided tours of the desert for foreigners. Such tourists nowadays often stay with the desert nomads like this."

Desi was enchanted. A tall moustachioed man of impressive bearing and impregnable dignity bent to offer her a silver basin and a bar of soap, poured water over her hands as she washed, then gave her a weather-beaten square of cloth to dry them.

"Is this a work camp?" she asked. "Why are there no women?"

"Women do not serve strangers," Salah said. "In the morning probably some will come and show you their craft work."

"Lovely! What sort of things do they make?"

"Dolls, pottery, maybe. You will have to wait and see."

Very soon food was laid before them.

"Is it the desert air, or is this food totally delicious?" Desi demanded, falling on it with a reckless abandon that she would have to pay for by eating starvation rations soon.

"We haven't eaten since lunch," Salah pointed out mildly.

"Yes, but I'm so used to going without food, it shouldn't get to me like this," Desi said. "I've been eating far too much since I got here; at this rate I'll have to fast completely for a week!"

"Not on this trip, please. The desert is dangerous enough without that."

Desi nodded, taking his point, and consciously slowed her eating.

"They use so much oil!" she protested. "In the palace, too. Is that what makes it so flavourful? How on earth does everybody in this country not turn into an elephant?"

Salah laughed aloud. "Olive oil," he corrected her, as if he were talking about gold. "Olive oil is very healthy, as well as giving its delicious flavour to food. We grow our own species of olive. Barakati olive oil is rare but very prized in the world, and very little is exported. Its flavour is excellent."

When the last of the food had been presented, they were politely left with only each other and the stars. Above them a shooting star rushed along a golden pathway to oblivion.

Suddenly the night air was heavy around them, weighted with awareness. And now that there was nothing to cloak it, their hungry need rose up like heat from the sand to cloud the space between them.

"They are preparing our tent," Salah said, his voice low and hoarse. "Will you sleep with me, tonight, Desi? I want you."

Eleven

Her heart leapt with yearning, her body melted into instant need. But she looked at him for a moment, resisting, remembering his harsh words earlier in the day.

"Tell me what it means to you, that you want me," she said quietly.

"It means you are a beautiful, sensual woman."

"Not good enough. Next answer."

"What do you want to hear?"

"You've thought yourself too good to talk to me for something like ten years. Now you're sleeping with me. Have you looked at that fact?"

"Is this why you came? To prove something to me?" he asked.

"My interest in proving anything to you runs in the minus figures, Salah. I find that when a person makes an accusation, he's usually talking to a mirror. Are you trying to prove something to me?"

"You forget that I did not go to your country. You came to mine."

"You forget that I did not go to your bed. You came to mine."

"Why did you come out to me? You came to me. You knew I was waiting."

"I think we've agreed the old sexual fire still has live coals amongst the ashes," Desi said. "Still, I don't call stepping out of my room to get some air 'coming to you', exactly."

"You called my name. You knew I was there."

"I didn't, actually. Why were you there?"

"You know it," he said.

"Closure, you say. What do you need closure on, exactly, Salah? Because you look as though you've had closure on everything in life. You look as if you've shut down everything except the food intake. What's left?"

He put out one hand to catch her chin and turned her head. For one tremulous moment his eyes met hers.

"You know what is left."

Honeyed sweetness flooded up her body, making her neck weak.

"You stirred up what was frozen, Desi. Until you came, I had forgotten how much I once loved you."

"Salah!" she whispered.

"And how little you loved me."

"You think?" she said bitterly.

"You did not love me at all. You said so, and you were right."

"I was sixteen!"

"Yes. You were young. I also was young, too young for such powerful feelings. I could not control what I felt. You said I was like the Kaljuks, and my only thought, Desi, was to prove to you that I could never be like them."

"Is that why you joined Prince Omar?" she breathed, horrified.

He shrugged. "I was running across a rocky ledge, looking for a way down to a Kaljuk gun emplacement that had been shelling a mountain town for a week." Unconsciously he stroked the scar that ran across his cheekbone to above his ear. "There was an explosion of light in my head, that's all I remember. I woke up in the hospital.

"You were there with me day and night, Desi. You were my solace and my torment, in one. I dreamed of you, sleeping and waking. I wanted you more than anything in the world. I begged you to come to me. You did not come."

"I tried, but Leo…" Immediately she wished she hadn't pronounced the name.

"Yes, Leo," he said in a different tone. "Sami sent me a letter with pictures of you in your new life with this old man. Then I understood. You did not love me, you could never be mine. I wrote you the letter to tell you I knew it.

"But I could not defend myself against the knowing. It went straight into my heart. The pain was like the end of the world, Desi. I did not recover, not even after I told myself I did. When you love someone the way I loved you…. Every day and every night I yearned for you. In the bed of other women, I dreamed of you."

Suddenly she had to choke back tears.

"Why did you never tell me? Never try to get in touch?" she demanded. "It was up to you, wasn't it? After that letter did you expect me to try to contact you again?"

"No," he said. "I expected nothing. You were with Leo. My love died, a terrible, painful death that I thought had killed my heart.

"One day, I awoke from the pain. But still I was not free of you. Then it was the memory of love itself that haunted me. Fool that I was, I wanted to find this feeling again, with another woman. I thought you could be wiped from my memory forever and I would feel alive again.

"But that is impossible, I learned that. I can never feel such an impact again. I don't know why it is so, but it is. I was ten times a fool to wish it. Such love is weakness. An addiction."

He paused, but she had no words.

"I thought it was dead, Desi. Before you came I thought there was nothing left, not even ashes. When my father told me he would let you come, I was angry, that was all. I thought, it is over. What business does she have, to come to me now?

"Then you came, and it was not what I expected. Anger was only the first of many feelings. I understood things I did not understand before.

"Our love and its death has affected every decision of my life from that moment, every breath I took, every woman I rejected as a wife. I understand it now."

"God," she whispered. Her heart was choking her.

"I want to free myself, Desi. My parents urge me to get married—for ten years they have wanted this. Now even I see it is time. But I can't go to my future wife with such a burden of the past. Not now that I feel its weight."

Her mouth opened in a soundless gasp as she took in his meaning.

"It is time to leave this behind. We have a few days together. I want to finish with these broken hopes. I want to bury the past once and forever. I want to go to my new wife with a heart free and ready to accept her."

She was silent, struggling with feeling. A sound like gunshot startled her as one of the flaming torches fell to be extinguished in the sand, and its dying spark shot skyward like a soul going home.

"And how will sleeping with me for a few days free your heart?" she asked at last.

"I have been haunted by you, Desi, by the memory of lovemaking that moved the earth. Nothing has matched it, but it is because nothing can match it. You can't match a dream. It is a fantasy, I know it, born from the fact that you were my first experience of love."

She wanted to tell him how it had been for her. The tearing grief, the bottomless yearning for that soul-deep connection, the determination to forget. Then Leo's terrible betrayal, and afterwards, the emptiness, the feeling that that part of her had died. And the terrible shock, seeing Salah again, to discover that it might still be there.

"I want that haunting to stop. Can you understand this? And I think—to put out my hand and know that it *is* you, and that the sex is what it is and no more—then I can close the book. I want to close it, Desi."

"You're going to marry my best friend, feeling like this?" she protested.

"Don't you see, it is not feeling? It is a memory, that is all."

"What if it worked the other way? What if this revived your love? Then what?"

Salah shook his head. "Do not fear for me, Desi."

"And what about my feelings? They don't matter?"

He was silent, his eyes meeting hers. He didn't believe she had any feelings to be hurt, that was obvious. And she just could not open her mouth to tell him. What would he do with such knowledge?

"You're sure this is not a disguised desire to punish me?" she pressed.

"How would this punish you?"

"You might think I'm vulnerable. You suspect me of coming here to see you. What did you imagine I wanted?"

An odd expression crossed his face in torchlight. "What power do I have to hurt you?"

Before she could answer, one of the Bedouin came and spoke to him.

"Our tent is ready," Salah said. "Come to bed."

And in spite of everything, her heart kicked with cell-deep anticipation.

The interior of the tent was softly lighted in the glow of two hurricane lamps. The earth was covered with reed mats and carpets, the space was divided into two sections by curtains of mosquito netting. On one side there was a large basin and two jugs of water behind a curtain. The other side held cushions and a thin mattress spread with a clean striped cloth.

A small spade was placed discreetly by the entrance, and Desi picked it up and went out to walk into the dunes. When she returned Salah had washed and was behind the netting, zipping their sleeping bags into a double. He turned and looked at her, and suddenly she was remembering the night they had spent in a little cabin on the island. Then, too, they had lit hurricane lanterns.

Then, too, the air between them had been thick with anticipation, and her limbs had been heavy with it.

They did not speak. He got up and went out.

Desi got out her sponge bag and went into the little space to bathe. She had packed unperfumed soap, to avoid enticing insects, but now she wished she could risk using some scent. Nor could the cotton pyjamas she had packed be called anything but plain.

She knew she was being a fool. She was storing up heart-break for herself.

But if for Salah lovemaking was a necessary way of coming to terms with the past, for her it was thirst in the desert.

All those years of telling herself it had been nothing to him. That if he had truly loved her, he could never have written what he did. What he told her this evening was like a firestorm in her. He *had* loved her.

If she had known that, would she have had the courage to write back, to shout at him for his despicable attitude? To fight?

But how could she have been happy with a man who harboured such alien, archaic views? Would he ever have treated her as an equal? A man makes love to a virgin and then calls her a slut? When she looked at it squarely, she knew she had had a lucky escape.

If only it felt like that.

When Salah returned to the tent, she was lying in the sleeping bag reading by the light of one of the lanterns. She looked up.

He stood gazing at her from the other side of the heavy netting, a shadowy silhouette, tall and powerful in a flowing robe, perfectly still. For a moment, as they stared at each other, the world stopped. There was no past between them, no future, the silence whispered, there was only the moment. Then he lifted the netting and stepped inside her little cocoon.

The little slow intake of her breath as she watched him was perfectly audible in the silence. Rivulets of anticipation coursed through her. She put down her book.

Lamplight caressed his curling black hair like melted gold. His desert cloak was open. She took in the vision of a flat, hard stomach, snug boxers, legs that were powerfully muscled. So different, and yet still there was the shadow of the eager young body that she had first seen so long ago.

A thin pale mark ran from his abdomen, over one hip and down his thigh almost to the knee. That was the line that marked the frontier between then and now: his battle scars.

He had a light dusting of hair on his forearms as well as a neat mat of chest hair. A delicate line of black curls tracing the middle of his abdomen gathered momentum as it reached his shorts. His flesh stirred as he looked at her.

It was unmistakably, primitively male.

And primally, powerfully erotic. She could not remember a time when the mere sight of a man's body had affected her so deeply, drawing her irresistibly.

Salah shrugged off the robe and dropped it on the carpet. His shoulders looked even more powerful now. He sank down onto his haunches, and then he was beside her, his mouth searching for hers, his heat enveloping her.

Her hand went of its own accord to the flesh at his groin, and she stroked him hungrily as it turned to marble, drunk on the knowledge that her touch had such power over him. She had seen statues of gods with erect sex, and tonight she understood the primitive urge to worship such flesh.

His head fell back at the assault of pleasure, and she slipped her fingers inside the elastic of his waistband, to draw the black fabric down and off his body. Then he lay naked in glowing lamplight, his eyes watching her with a black fury of need that stirred her to the depths. Her hand enclosed him again, and she bent down over him and almost without conscious volition, because in some deep part of her she was compelled to it, took him into her mouth.

His breath caught, and the sound shivered over her skin. She closed her eyes and gave herself up to the pleasure of giving pleasure. She felt his hands in her hair, cupping her head, felt the intensity of his need.

"Too much," he said hoarsely after a few moments. His hands moved to catch her shoulders, and he drew her up into a fierce embrace. "Too much." He leaned away from her for a moment, she heard the puff of his breath, and then the tent was in darkness.

In another moment, she was wrapped in his embrace.

Twelve

The haunting sound of a distant *muezzin* woke her. Desi slipped out of bed, leaving Salah still sleeping, wrapped herself in her bathrobe, and went out.

The sky was showing the first signs of morning, the moon palely giving way to her ferocious brother as the sky paled. The air was deliciously fresh and crisp. Beneath her feet the sand was cool. When she dug at it with her toes, the layer underneath proved to be still warm, as if the earth were a living creature and she had burrowed under its fur. She stood, shivering a little, her feet warm in the sand, savouring the lonely sound of the *muezzin*'s voice against the utter peace of the desert, until it fell silent.

Then she took the spade and went into the dunes. When she returned, the camp was beginning to stir.

It was her first desert dawn, and Desi was moved by its perfection. She went back into the tent to discover Salah up and gone, and the pitchers filled with fresh water. She hurried with her washing and dressing, not to miss a minute of the morning.

When she got outside again, dressed in khaki shorts and a t-shirt but still barefoot, the sky was the colour of smoke, with a straggle of cloud and a swathe of rich, deep pink at the horizon. She set off running. Overhead slowly the sky revealed itself as blue, while above the horizon the pink expanded into red, gold and yellow, setting the cloud alight, and a tiny burning arc of fire appeared behind the dunes.

She jogged out towards the camel corral, where the beasts regarded her with placid condescension as she passed, and up the steep side of a nearby dune, her feet sinking deep into the sand, which brought her to the top breathless.

She stood looking out over the vista as the newborn sun painted the tops of the dunes in bright gold. The camp was revealed as a few broad, low tents pitched around a small central area where a pit had been dug to form a brazier. A man was stirring the coals into life.

Not far away from the camp, women were drawing water from the concrete housing of a well. In the light wind of morning their brightly patterned robes and scarves fanned out against a backdrop of endless pale sand. A herd of white and black goats clustered around, eagerly pushing towards the broad troughs that the women were filling. Their bleating was the only sound on the morning air, a dozen different pitches and rhythms like strange music.

The women were covertly watching her. From her vantage point on the dune she waved, and two of the older women smiled, one of them shyly waggling her hand at chest height. The younger ones drew their scarves up to cover their mouths and dropped their eyes.

Back in the tent, she found Salah, looking handsome and

intimidating in desert robes, seated lotus-position on the ground, consulting a map. When she came in, fresh-faced with her exercise and the morning chill, he looked up and smiled. Her breath caught with surprise. It was the first time she had seen him so relaxed. The frown was gone from his eyes.

"Ready for breakfast?" he asked.

"Ravenous! Is it going to be local fare again, or do they provide the usual tourist stuff?" she asked as he led her outside to where someone had placed a carpet for them with cushions side by side in the sun. A man in flowing robes and turban was setting down plates.

"They aren't so changed yet. The few travellers they see are still the sort who want to experience what the world has to offer, not impose their own lifestyle on it. We will be offered the best of their own food."

"Can't wait!"

As last night, the only utensils were spoons, and again she washed her hands under the stream of water poured for her from a ewer.

Little bowls of yoghurt and a curious mud-coloured paste were set before them and Desi was negotiating with the yoghurt when the pièce de résistance arrived: a huge, deliciously sizzling, buttery, puffy pancake that had been grilled over charcoal. Something that looked suspiciously like honey was drizzled all over it.

On the pure desert air the scent of it was tantalizing.

"Oh, *totally* too fattening! I must remember to ask before I go around demanding the local food," Desi exclaimed helplessly.

"You can eat all the yoghurt." Salah grinned and tore off a large chunk of the pancake, expertly rolling it up in one hand before taking a bite. Honey dripped onto his lower lip and he licked it off, his eyes closing with enjoyment.

He turned his head and looked at her from under lowered eyelids. "Hot. Sweet." *Like you.*

The thought of what those long, strong fingers, his tongue and mouth had done to her last night stormed through her. Her neck was suddenly too weak to hold up her head.

She took a hasty mouthful of the yoghurt and shivered as a blast of sourness reached her nerves. "I give in!" she cried, reaching to tear off a bit of the pancake and dipping the end in a little pool of honey that had collected in the lower levels of its bubbly terrain.

"Delicious! That's so yummy it should be classed as a dangerous weapon! Is every meal over the next few days going to be diet sabotage?"

"Boiled camel feet sometimes lack that certain something," he advised. "Eat while you can."

"Between the suntan and the fat, my agent will kill me."

"Start a fashion for voluptuous," he suggested.

"You don't understand. I *am* voluptuous. I abandoned the waif figure years ago. Do you think this body is Size Zero? Think again."

"What is Size Zero?"

"That's the size models try to be. I'd have to lose ten or twelve pounds to get there. As a model I'm considered borderline fat, as my agent keeps warning me."

Salah stared at her for a moment, then began to laugh. It started as a chuckle, but quickly descended to his belly, where it took on a deeply contagious quality that drew her irresistibly into laughter too. With great gusts and hoops, they were caught so helplessly that finally Salah fell backwards into the sand.

She turned to look down at him, at the black curls dusted with sand, sun-crinkled eyes, white teeth and laughing mouth. A new expression came into his eyes, and the laughter died on her lips.

He lifted his hand up her back and clenched it in her hair.

"You are perfectly beautiful," he said, and for an uncharted time they were still, gazing at each other through ten long, wasted years.

Then Salah's eyes widened in something like alarm. His face became shuttered and he sat up.

"It is time to leave," he said flatly. And only then did Desi breathe again.

As he had predicted, several of the older women were sitting near the camel corral as they left, with their crafts and other wares spread out for examination.

Desi crouched down in front of the spread. Dolls made of bits of cloth and coloured thread, stones with fossils embedded in them, some pottery bowls with a curious design, and, best of all, some beautifully etched and painted bits of camel bone.

Desi oohed and aahed over everything, miming her admiration, and, unable to disappoint such dignified, open people, who clearly were very poor, carefully chose several items.

The camel bone work was exquisite: carved and engraved rings and pendants, and little etched scenes on flat strips of bone that looked for all the world like ivory.

Desi picked up an oval medallion bearing a delicately etched camel. Brown paint had been rubbed into the etched lines, so the outlines were dark against a smudged paler background blending into the creamy white of the bone.

"This stuff is gorgeous!" she said over her shoulder to Salah. "Where did she learn to carve like this?"

Salah briefly spoke with the artist, a middle-aged and weather-beaten woman with a thin face and calloused, graceful hands.

"She learned it from her father. He learned it from his own

father, and as none of her brothers survived childhood, he taught her. Her father used to colour such etchings in many colours, but she can no longer find the substances to make the paints, so she paints mostly in monochrome. She misses having the colours and apologizes because the work is not very pretty."

"It's lovely. Can you find out her name for me, please?"

As Desi drew out her wallet, one of the women signalled to her, then opened a bit of cloth to show her something.

A small clay statue of a woman with a large tiara and hair exquisitely moulded in tumbling curls down her back and over her shoulder. She had prominent breasts, and her pubic hair was clearly marked, but her body had been given a dress of paler clay that flaked easily when she picked it up.

Desi examined it curiously.

"How old is this?" she asked.

"'Very, very old'," Salah translated for the women.

"Do you think that's true? I mean, if so, wouldn't it be in a museum?"

"It is unlikely that anyone in this tribe would make a forgery of that kind. They would consider it blasphemous. That is why they have given her a modest cover-up before selling her."

Forgery or not, Desi was taken by the little figure.

"How much is it?"

Again a short colloquy. "Twenty dirhams."

Desi blinked. "But it must—it has to be a forgery. If it were genuine they'd be asking a lot more, wouldn't they?"

"They find such things in the sand as they travel. They used to destroy them, thinking them some sort of witchcraft. Then they learned that foreigners liked them. For them, twenty dirhams is a lot of money, especially for a found item. They don't understand why tourists like things that are old and broken like this."

"Well, I certainly like her."

When she had paid and everything had been wrapped in rags or bits of old newspaper and put in a very distressed plastic bag, she thanked the women and got to her feet. With many goodbyes they were on their way.

"Where do they spend the money?" she asked later, as they headed out over the desert.

"Taxis sometimes come and take them to town."

"What, such a distance?"

He flicked her a look. "They are not always camped so far from civilisation. But mostly they buy from the travelling shops—trucks loaded with every kind of merchandise, which service the nomad communities."

"But no chance for that artist to buy manufactured paints?"

"Probably not."

"If I found her some paints, would there be a way to send them to her?"

After a short silence, Salah asked, "Why do you bother with this?"

"Because she's an artist, and art this good has a right to the proper materials. Are you going to answer my question?"

"If you sent her something, eventually it would find its way to her. Tell me, when did you develop an interest in the indigenous art and antiquities of Barakat?"

"I do a lot of travelling in my job, Salah. Half the time I don't get to see anything more than the inside of my five star hotel and the shoot site. It's not the art so much as the people. I rarely get to meet real people in a real environment. Those women are lovely people, so friendly, and they look as though they can use the money."

"But the goddess is a collectors' item. Are you a collector?"

"The goddess? Is that who she is? How do you know?" Her

interest sparked, Desi dug into the bag of goodies and unwrapped the little clay statuette. She held it cupped in her hand.

"What's her name?"

"It depends on where she was found. It's almost impossible to say with certainty. My father would say, a love or fertility goddess."

Desi frowned, accessing recent memories. "Inanna! Wasn't she the Goddess of Love?"

Salah flicked her a look and said gravely, "In Sumer. Yes."

"Could it be her?"

"You would have to ask my father."

"Oh, but it's impossible. It would mean this was five thousand years old!"

"It probably is."

Desi gasped. A feeling of wonder flooded her, and a strange energy, as if the little goddess's locked-up power had suddenly been released into her palm.

"That's amazing," she whispered. "But—why…I mean, how is it I can buy something so valuable just like that?"

"She might be taken away from you at the airport."

"Really?"

"It is illegal to take antiquities out of the Barakat Emirates. It is part of our cultural heritage. We have museums where such pieces belong."

"Seems a pretty poor way to manage resources. Wouldn't it be better to stop the sale in the first place?"

"We can't police the entire desert. Instead tourists are searched before they leave, and such valuable items as your little goddess are confiscated. This discourages tourists from making such purchases in future."

She laughed. "So I'll have to give up my little talisman?"

"Not everything is found, of course. Perhaps less than

forty percent. If you pack it carefully, you might get away with it."

She looked at him quizzically. "What makes you think I would want to 'get away with' taking something that belongs in the country's museums?"

"You seem to like it."

"You think I steal everything I like? Have you noticed me wearing any of the Crown Jewels?"

"You paid for it. Most people would not consider it theft."

"Oh, give me a break! We make love at night, and in the morning you salve your conscience by suggesting I'm dishonourable, is that it? We've been there before, Salah, and I got enough of it last time. Can't you just enjoy the sex for what it is and leave your condemnation in your pocket?"

His jaw tightened. "No, that is not it. I apologize. In my work I see many people who consider themselves honest but who are without any conscience at all in this area."

"In your work?"

"One of my areas as Cup Companion is antiquities security."

"Say what?"

"My task is to prevent the smuggling of antiquities to foreign markets. Both West and East have many wealthy men who are interested in the ancient cultures of the Barakat Emirates. Organizers pay what to poor nomads and farmers seems a good price for any artefact they can steal or dig up, then sell them on to unscrupulous dealers for many times more. They in turn sell it on. By the time it reaches the collector, he is paying thousands of times the sum the finder got. Our heritage is in danger of being destroyed by this practice."

"Are you saying your personal mission is to stop it? How do you go about it?"

"In various ways, none of them satisfactory. People mostly rob the sites of ancient cities and settlements which have not yet been studied, near the villages where they live. It is a big problem for archaeologists like my father. As you know, once something is dug up and removed, its provenance can never be discovered. So even if we recover that piece, its historic value is lost."

"Of course." Archaeologists must know exactly where something is found before it can shed light on history: Desi had learned that in her researches. A jug was just a jug unless you knew what else it was found with, its period, of what civilisation it had formed a part.

"But theft is not my father's biggest worry."

There was something in his tone that caught her attention.

"Really? What is, then?"

"The answer is in your hand."

She thought it was a covert challenge, that he wanted to know if she had any real archaeological interest or understanding. She held up the little statue.

Goddess of love. What did she know about the goddess of love? Worshipped as the one who made animals and land, as well as humans, fertile. Her sexual characteristics painted over by whoever had found it, because now her blatant sexuality was seen not as powerful, but immodest.

"Oh my God!" Desi whispered.

Found in a land where to worship the divine in any form but as Allah was blasphemy.

"Tell me I'm wrong!" she begged. "Is your father afraid that religious fanatics might...oh, no!"

"There is a significant risk. My father thinks the site is a city devoted to a love goddess. It could rewrite history. But if the Kaljuks and their supporters here in the Barakat Emirates hear of this find, and learn where it is located, the risk is worse than ordinary theft—they may try to sabotage the site itself. They would want to destroy it completely."

Desi's strongest emotion after dismay was exasperation. "For God's sake! Four thousand years before Islam even happened!"

"They do not care about that." Salah slowed the vehicle and turned his head, and his black eyes found hers. "That is why, Desi, I ask you if you have any other reason for wanting to visit this dig."

"What?" she asked blankly.

"If someone has asked you to try to find out what you can about the site my father is digging, you must understand that it is unlikely to be for genuine academic purposes."

"What are you trying to say?" She blinked at him.

His voice was rough now, his eyes probing.

"I know you are not here for the reason you have given. Do not be the innocent tool of villains, Desi. If someone wants to know about this project, it is because they want to steal our history from us, one way or the other. Tell me who asked you to use your connection with our family in this way."

She felt as if he had slapped her. She had to open her mouth twice before she could speak.

"What do you imagine you're talking about?" she cried. "No one asked me to visit the dig! No one asked me to come here!"

"This is not the truth, Desi! Tell me their names! Such information can be invaluable to us."

"I am not anyone's tool, innocent or otherwise!" she cried indignantly. "Do you imagine I could be so stupid? Or maybe you think I'm the cheat myself? Is that what you think?"

"Why are you here?"

"I told you why!"

He was silent, watching the guarded look come into her eyes. The lie was in her tone; even she could hear it. But she had to glare back at him with the best outrage she could muster.

"I am not anybody's tool," she insisted, hating the expression on his face, hating the lie she was living. How she wished she could throw the truth at his head.

He said, "I will take you to my father, if you insist, Desi. But I tell you now that you will not learn where the site is, even though you see it with your own eyes—the desert does not tell the uninitiated where they are. You will learn no village name. Do you still wish to make the journey?"

"Of course I do!" she cried. "And I couldn't care less about knowing the compass coordinates! You can blindfold me if you want to. That's not why I want to visit the site. I told you—I had no idea how important it was till you told me the other day. I thought it was just another site. I had no idea I was asking for such a big favour."

"My father could not say no."

"Well, I'm sorry. I wish I'd known."

"And now that you do?"

With every fibre of her being she wanted to say, *forget it! I don't want anything from you or your father.*

But she couldn't. She said lamely, "Well, aren't we nearly halfway there now?"

He nodded without speaking.

"Salah, I swear to you I am not here to steal any secrets for anybody."

He looked at her as if there was nothing in the world he wanted more than to believe her. But when he said, "Good," she knew he was still doubting.

"You always did judge me," she reminded him bitterly.

"Not without cause."

"Then, as now, the cause was all in your own head."

He laughed, seemed about to say something, then changed his mind.

For one powerful, compelling moment Desi had the conviction that she should confide everything to Salah—should just tell him *Samiha doesn't want to marry you, she's in love with someone else.*

She half opened her mouth and closed it again. If she were wrong, she would not be the one to suffer.

Or at least, not more than was already on the cards.

Thirteen

That day was spent crossing the bleakest imaginable desert, emptier than she could ever have dreamed. For miles they saw nothing but sand and rock. No animals, no trees, not even any scrub.

The sun was scorching. The landcruiser was air-conditioned, but that did not stop the sun coming through the windows, and setting her skin on fire. Desi had always loved heat, but this was something else. There was no shade anywhere, it was hour after hour of burning sand, till her eyes grew hypnotized and her brain tranced.

She would not protest or complain, because she suspected he was waiting for just that. Nor did she want to give him any excuse for turning back. *It'll be hell on wheels, Desi,* Sami had said, but even she could not have foreseen this.

Desi lifted the bottle of water to her lips for the fiftieth time that day, and took a long swig. She'd never drunk so much water in her life.

"I suppose if we ran out of gas or water out here, we'd be dead in an hour," she observed mildly.

"It would take longer than that. But we will not run out," Salah said.

At noon they stopped only briefly to eat and drink. Salah, wearing his desert robe and the headscarf she had learned to call *keffiyeh,* got out to stretch, but Desi remained in the vehicle. To step outside in this heat would be tantamount to suicide, or at the very least, instant second degree burn. She had put on shorts and a t-shirt in the nomad camp this morning, and now she was sorry. But it was too much effort to think of changing into something with sleeves.

After only fifteen minutes they were on their way again.

In late afternoon Salah pointed through the windscreen. "We'll camp there," he said.

Desi frowned and shaded her eyes till she saw it: a large outcrop of sand-coloured stone ahead. She would not have seen it if he hadn't pointed it out. The best way to see anything out here was by the shadow it cast, and there was no shadow.

"Will there be some shade? Why can't I see a shadow?" She was desperate to be out of the sun.

"On the other side. The sun is behind us now."

"Are we heading east?" Desi frowned and looked at the sun. They were. She hadn't noticed him change direction. "Why?"

Salah glanced at her ruefully. "I'm sorry. I overshot. We should have reached it an hour ago."

"Thus the great desert navigator whose ancestors survived to produce him!"

"As long as the mistakes are not fatal, of course, one survives."

"You can't imagine how comforting."

At least they could laugh.

Ten minutes later—how deceiving distances were when

you had no real landmarks!—they reached it. The mound was much bigger than she had imagined, a small hill, the size of a substantial building. And Salah slowed the Land Cruiser and pulled around to the other side, Desi gasped in relief.

"An oasis!" she cried. "A real, true blue oasis!"

"At this season the water will be brackish."

Two dozen palm trees surrounded a large pool of water in the rock's welcome shadow.

"Heaven is a relative construct, I see," Desi said.

Salah pulled the vehicle up underneath a rock overhang and Desi tumbled out.

Even in the shade it was boiling hot. She gasped. "Wow! How right you were about travelling in this heat! Is it all going to be like this?"

"No," he said, opening the back and beginning to unload supplies. When Desi moved to help him he waved her away. "Leave it to me for now. You are too hot. Go and sit in the shade."

He was right there, and she could assume he was more used to this heat than she. She sank down on a rock and watched him heave out the tent.

"I think I've drunk four litres of water today! Do we have enough?"

"We have plenty. When did you last take a salt tablet?"

She told him, and he nodded approval.

She knew she must be sweating, but she'd never have known it by her skin. In such dry air, sweat seemed to evaporate before you saw it.

"I suppose this is as good as a detox cure," Desi mused.

When Salah had unloaded the equipment and supplies, he slammed the tailgate and turned to look into the sun.

With his eyes narrowed, his chiselled face outlined by sun and shadow, he looked fiercely handsome, a face from another century. Desi felt lightheaded, almost drunk, with his beauty.

"You're the image of the desert," she said dreamily.

Salah flicked her a glance. "You need food," he said.

He bent to pick up the roll that was the tent, and carried it to a flat spot among the trees. Desi set down her bottle, dusted her hands on her butt, and moved to help him.

An hour later the tent was up, the sleeping bags unrolled, and Desi was watching the sun go down to glory over the desert as she scooped up the last morsel of lamb and aubergine stew.

"Does this place have a name?" she asked dreamily.

"It is called Halimah's Rest."

"Halimah? Didn't you tell me she was a great queen or something?"

"Yes. After her husband's death, she held the throne for her son against all comers for years."

"What was she doing out here in the middle of nowhere?"

"Queen Halimah and her army got lost during a battle. A local Bedouin boy led her to this oasis. The army camped here and refreshed themselves and went on to win the battle the next day. Later Halimah commanded that the pool be banked with brick and a well dug, to the great benefit of the Bedouin. You can still see the remnants of the brick walls."

"Who was she fighting with?"

"Adil ibn Bilah, her dead husband's nephew, who wanted to take the throne from her."

"He didn't succeed?"

"No. He was killed, and Halimah made an example of his generals. No one challenged her rule for some time afterwards."

The sun was all but gone now. Salah got up and moved among the trees, collecting palm leaves and bark. Desi sat and watched the desert change from gold to red and then to purple.

The desert went on forever. A sense of unreality settled over her. What stories the sand whispered to the secret ear!

"This is so weird," she murmured, after a long silence.

"What?" Salah began laying a fire with what he had collected.

"I feel as though I've plugged into a mindset that's been sitting here forever. As if time is nothing, only the desert exists."

"The desert has many effects on the mind. You've never been in the desert before?"

"I've done a couple of photo shoots in the more obvious places. Golden beaches and palm trees. Once we went out to an old battlefield and I posed by burnt-out tanks. That was horrible. But never right out in the middle of nowhere, never where the desert could really get to you. Never anywhere I felt like this."

"There is more than one sort of mirage," Salah said, setting a match to the fire.

"Meaning?"

"People see what they want to see in the desert."

"And what do I want to see?"

"That in the desert time is transcended, perhaps. That time does not matter."

She went still with the truth of it. There was silence between them, and then, as if driven, he went on.

"If there is only the desert and eternity, how can ten years matter? Do you yearn for that time of innocence, Desi? I, too. We drive across the desert together, and I know that, if only we had been more *thabet*—what word is it?—stead…steady…"

"Stea—" Her throat closed. She cleared it. "Steadfast."

Darkness was settling around them as the first stars appeared. Thick, roiling smoke curled up from under the stacked leaves, and then a puff of yellow flame.

"Steadfast, yes. We might still be here together, but how different it would be. You would be my wife. Our children would sleeping in the tent. Do you feel their ghosts, Desi, as I do?"

Baba, baba, I want a drink!

Her heart convulsed at the nearness of the dream. Desi opened her mouth to breathe.

"What is there in that moment that still traps us, after so many years?" he pressed. "A few weeks out of a lifetime. Why is it so close?"

The question hung on the air like smoke, symbol of the fire that lurked beneath.

Desi moved her head. Something burned her eyes and the back of her throat. "I don't know." The desert at night was like nothing she had ever experienced, and yet there was something about the campfire, the stars and his nearness that brought those island feelings close. Love—the *memory* of love! she corrected herself—tore at her heart.

A moment later he was beside her on the blanket, his voice hoarse and low.

"Here there is no time, Desi. You feel it. I feel it. Time has disappeared. Here we can be what we were. Let us make love once more as the innocent children we were. Let us remember the love we felt, just once; let us make love as if ten years had not passed, as if you had come to me then."

Her heart was caught between melting and breaking. A sob burned her throat. "What do you want, Salah?"

She felt the approach of heat, and then his hand was on her breast, cupping it tenderly.

"Do you remember the first time I touched you, Desi? How my hand trembled. Let me touch you like that again."

Slowly he drew the loose shirt down her arms and tossed it to one side. Under her t-shirt she was naked, the heat was too much for a bra, and he knew it. Gently he pushed her down onto the blanket, his hand slipping up under the thin cotton to find the silky curve of her breast and encircle it as if coming home.

"The first time I touched you like this, Desi, how my blood leapt! The magic of your soft breast, the way your flesh answered me—" he stroked his palm over the shivered, hungry tip that responded to his urgency with aching need, then pushed the cloth up and bent his head.

The firelight shadowed his chiselled face, showed her the tortured passion in his eyes, so that she could almost believe he was again the boy he had been, passionate, loving, accepting, burning with need of her. She melted at the thought, body and soul, and as his lips gently encircled her flesh, she whispered his name, as she had so long ago.

Salah.

Her voice held the surprise of awakening passion, as if he heard it down the years and she were still a virgin, and he closed his eyes as the power of it struck him a blow straight to the heart.

As they had then, his hands became urgent, his tenderness struggling with the need that moved in them both. He pushed the t-shirt over her head and off, and his eyes devoured the beauty of her perfect breasts, her skin's creamy smoothness caressed by the flickering blaze that stroked her even as his hands did. Then he was jealous, primitively jealous of the fire's adoration of her, and moved over her, so that she lay in his shadow, as he urged off the shorts that had no right to touch her legs…

But starlight, too, adored her, glowing on her white forehead, her dampened lips. He bent to take possession there, too, his mouth hungry and urgent.

The hunger of years rose to her lips, and she opened her

mouth tenderly, willingly, hungrily, and as innocent now as then, for in the desert time disappears. Her hands wrapped him, fingers clenching on his shoulder, his head, clasping the rich black curls in the newness of that passion she had learned only with him. Each move of his mouth and tongue and lips was answered by hers, and his blood pounded through him and he struggled against the urgent need to take her, consume her, be one with her, now.

He shrugged out of his clothes, and then stretched out beside her, naked and gleaming in firelight. Her hands stroked the length of his chest and flank, and in the darkness and flickering shadow the honing of maturity and even his battle scar somehow were lost, so that his body was as fresh and perfect as at seventeen.

His fingers caressed her cheek, her temple, stroked the silky hair back from her brow as he gazed into eyes that reflected the night sky and all eternity. Stars glinted in her gaze as she smiled fearlessly, trustingly into his face, in a way no woman had done again. It touched him to the depths of his soul, and he gathered her wildly up in his arms, clumsy, inexperienced, like the boy he had been, and crushed her to him, drowned her mouth with his own, drank in the sweetness of her like wine.

His hands were strong, holding her as if he could never let her go, as they pressed her back, her shoulder, her head, desperate to bring her closer and closer, till she was part of him. She melted with yearning, with fulfilment, with need, crying her joy to the night air, to the desert that saw all, knew all.

His mouth drank and drank of the nectar of their kiss. Her body was pressed so tightly against him they were one flesh, and the hands that wrapped and caressed her sent sensation like honey through her, and in her response he felt the honey return and pour into his own flesh.

Still it was not enough for either; the last, the final union was still to come, and she began to plead with him as she had so long ago, soft murmurings in his ear that resonated in his heart, *please, Salah, please, please,* as she pressed closer and closer, as her body moulded to his and his to her.

He drew away a little then, unable to wait longer, for what they needed was to sink into each other, and remember who they had been.

He drew away, and his flesh fitted to hers with the hungry knowing of the key for the lock, and pushed inside, and they cried out together in surprise and completion, one voice that drenched their nerve ends with sweetness. And then they were locked together, gazing into each other's star-filled eyes, unmoving with the surprise of passion.

He stroked her face, her hair, she touched his full lips with a questing fingertip, and that moment of wonder and surprise was the same as it had been ten long years ago, that moment of feeling the pulse of an ancient rhythm burn up inside them, the summons of that urgent, age-old necessity that is the heartbeat of life. It began to move in them, through them, and they were helpless on the current of its urgency, the pulsing, pushing beat that took them closer and closer to the place where time is destroyed in eternity.

The fire watched greedily, coating their limbs with light and shadow, as they moved and embedded deeper and deeper into each other's being, towards the one.

They cried out as they approached it, cried their helpless pleasure, their consuming need, to all who would hear: earth and water and fire and air, and sky and time and nothingness and all, and then they were there, and all need, all urgency, exploded in a blaze of honeyed light that swept out from the tiny space where souls and bodies met, to enrich all creation. And, bathed in its glow, blinded by its brightness, for that place cannot be seen by mortal eyes, for one moment of perfection they cried out their gratitude, and then, slowly, because they must, sank back together into the abode of separation.

The firelight died, and still they lay entangled, unwilling to let the world enter between them again. But soon the desert chill invaded both body and soul.

"Now we know," said Salah, and there was something in his tone that chilled her even further, because it told her nothing had changed.

"Do we?"

"It was real," he said. "It was there. We destroyed it, but it was real."

"Is it better to know?" she asked bitterly, feeling somehow that it was tonight, not ten years ago, that she had created the real heartbreak for herself.

She stiffened to ward off pain, but Salah didn't answer. He sat up as night insects, drawn by the scent of honey, approached, and threw a few more dried fronds onto the dying blaze before disappearing down towards the pool, now shrouded in darkness.

Desi dug in her pack, got out her night gear and pulled it on, then sat there as smoke and flame curled up on the air, trying to see her way into the future.

He came out of the darkness like a pagan god, naked and strong, his body glistening with wet. As he pulled a towel out of his own pack and rubbed himself dry, she watched with detached admiration, as if at a work of art, until he had put on his night clothes and sat down again.

"Are you going to marry Sami?"

Salah shrugged and lifted a stick to stir the fire. "It is not agreed yet. But why not? I must marry someone."

"How can you talk about it so calmly? You know what love is. You remember how it feels. How can you contemplate marrying someone you don't love?"

In the firelight her eyes were dark, watching him. He turned his attention to the fire.

"The best love comes after marriage," he said. "You create a life together, and love each other within that life. It is easy to love the mother of your children."

"You don't sound convinced."

"I told you once, Desi!" he growled. "I will never love again in the way that I loved you. It is impossible. I do not wish it. It is better to marry in the old way—find your wife first, and then learn to love her. The other way is heartbreak."

Who had he first heard it from? His uncle? His grandfather? He couldn't remember now, but that it was wisdom his own life had proven. It was best to marry calmly. Strong feelings could always turn into their opposite.

They sat in silence for a few moments. "Is it because of your parents? Are they pressing you to marry?"

"I told you, my parents have been pressing me to marry for ten years. They have given up asking me. But they are right, it is time. I am nearly thirty. I am the eldest of my family."

"Why now? Why Sami?"

"There are reasons why a wife born and educated in the West is a good idea."

"What reasons?"

The moon was rising. Salah, his arms resting on his knees, gazed at her for a long moment. In firelight her face was hauntingly beautiful; no wonder that fingers of flame and shadow warred to caress it. He could not love her again, all that was past. But through the curls of smoke still she was a dream, a ten-year-old dream. And he could almost believe he was that boy again.

He must resist that temptation. The truth was elsewhere.

"Why do you ask these questions, Desi? What is it you want to know?"

"Because I don't believe it! Something doesn't add up."

"Why not?" He raised an eyebrow.

"I—I just think it's an extremely odd match, you and Sami. You're cousins!"

"By our tradition, that is the best match."

"But do you and Sami think so?"

"Some women raised abroad seek to retain connection with Barakat in this way. It means their children will have the right to citizenship in two countries. With the world so uncertain, that is not a bad thing."

"Is that what Sami wants?"

"Perhaps."

"And what about your own reasons?" she asked again.

He tossed something into the fire that crackled and sent sparks up to the treetops. "This comes at a time when I may have to move abroad and it will be best not to go on a diplomatic passport."

He felt her shock and wondered why it struck her so forcibly.

"You're going to be living in the West?" she gasped.

"Why not?"

"But you're a Cup Companion! Your life is here! At least—isn't it?"

"My duty is elsewhere, however. I did not become a Cup Companion for the privileges, but to do what is necessary for my prince and my country."

"And what duty requires you to move abroad?"

"This I cannot discuss with you, Desi."

"How long?"

"Why are you asking? Why do you want to know?" he

asked, and watched as her face closed. With distant anger, he wondered who had asked her to ask these questions, which he should not have answered. His guard was down.

Salah tossed the stick he was holding onto the fire.

"Let's get some sleep," he said.

Desi lay sleepless beside him long after his breathing told her Salah was out.

I still love him. I could tell him so. Ask him to love me again. The thought tortured her. She was half convinced that he was lying to himself when he said his love for her was dead. She, too, had believed herself immune, and how wrong she had been!

He wanted to move to the West. He wanted a Western wife. If she confessed the state of her heart might he pretend to love her for such a reason? At least he could be sure the sex was good. What if he thought, why not marry Desi, as easily as Sami?

Why not? whispered the voice of temptation.

Desi had never really understood what had motivated his letter. When the first flush of guilt and grief had passed, she had been almost sure that it was something to do with his illness. He had been shot in the head, she knew that. He'd been very ill for weeks. So for a long time she'd lived in hope that another letter would come, telling her he'd been delirious…but it never came.

But that was ten years ago. Why hasn't he got some distance on it? How can he still judge me the way he did? Is it just habit? Did he really never take it out and look at it? I'll talk to him tomorrow.

She must be careful. Because if what he really wanted, unconsciously or not, was to punish her for his inability to love another woman, she might offer him the perfect means. She was so vulnerable, yearning for his touch, melting at his nearness. How much more vulnerable she would be as his wife!

*But…*her heart whispered…*he's determined to love his wife, whoever she is. If he could love me again…he's planning to live in the West, who knows for how long? Maybe we could live in two worlds. It's doable.*

She argued with herself while the moon tracked her serene path across the heavens, and came to no conclusion.

Fourteen

They were up before the sun. Desi bathed in the oasis pool, but the water left her skin feeling sticky, and afterwards she rinsed as best she could in a tiny ration of bottled water. Still feeling slightly grubby, she got into clean white cargo pants and a loose long-sleeved white shirt, hoping by this means to keep the heat off better than yesterday. She stuffed her hair up under her straw hat and felt a welcome morning breeze caress the back of her neck.

What she'd give for a shower!

Just before noon the desert monotony was broken by distant rocky hills and a long line of green on the horizon. Mount Shir towered above the scene, remote and majestic. They must have been travelling north for some time, but she had been too involved with her thoughts to notice.

"What's that green I see?" she asked.

"That is Wadi Daud."

"Wadi—does that mean *oasis?*"

"Wadi means a valley, or a riverbed, where there is water only in the rainy season. But Wadi Daud has underground water and there is an irrigation project there, so it is green all year round. Not so green now as it will be in a few months, but still pleasant."

Desi was surprised when a paved road appeared in front of them; she'd thought they were miles from such niceties. Salah turned onto it in a cloud of dust, and not long afterwards it slanted down into a broad, flat, rough-hewn valley with steep walls of purple-grey rock and a floor of green that stretched for miles in both directions. In the centre of the valley a stream trickled over a stony bed.

"In winter that is a torrent," Salah said. "In summer it often dries up completely."

Soon they were driving through palm and olive groves. Along on the other side of the valley she saw a small village amongst the greenery.

"Is that where we're headed?"

"I have friends who will give us lunch."

The house was like those she'd seen in the city: low, white and domed, set in the middle of a broad courtyard surrounded by a high white wall. A servant opened the outer door to them with a murmured "*Marhaban,*" and the blistering heat of the midday sun was instantly mitigated by the shade of numerous trees and the sound of a fountain.

A strikingly attractive woman with flashing black eyes and black curls cascading down her back came out of the house, smiling and calling what was obviously a warm greeting in Arabic. In a cotton summer dress, she had bare legs and feet; her arms were bare save for a few bracelets.

"Marhaban, marhaban jiddan, Salah! Nahnou…"

"Desi, Nadia," Salah said, just as Desi took off her hat to

wipe her forehead and her fair hair came tumbling down. "Desi doesn't speak Arabic, Nadia."

"Oh, I'm sorry!" Nadia's level gaze met hers with a frowning smile as the two women shook hands. "Hello, how are you? Welcome! You are very welcome! Salah, it's so good to see you!" she said. "Ramiz will be here in a minute. Come in, come in!"

She led them across the shady but still hot courtyard and into the cool of a large, airy room whose decor seemed to blend West and East, modern and ancient, with perfect ease. It was a massive, spreading space obviously covering most of one floor of the house, protected from the midday sun by green-covered canopies and thick walls.

The furniture was a mix of Western and Eastern, with conventional sofas and chairs and coffee tables in a cluster at one end, and cushions on a massive knotted silk carpet at the other.

The right hand wall had sliding glass doors looking out on to an obviously antique, mosaic-tiled pool with a fountain that reminded Desi of what she had seen at the palace. The left wall was a stunning row of pillars and delicately fluted arches through which could be seen an endless maze of pillars, arches, and mosaic floors, and the corner of a distant, sunny courtyard.

It took Desi a moment to realize that the entire scene was a *trompe l'oeil* painting. She was looking at a solid wall.

"This is spectacular!" she exclaimed involuntarily, stopping to gawp as Nadia, happily chatting to Salah, led them along the length of the room down to a sofa at the far end.

Nadia and Salah turned in surprise, then, seeing what had caught her, laughed.

"I love it, too," Nadia confessed with a smile. "You haven't seen it since it was finished, Salah, yes? That shows how long since you visited us! Anna finished it almost three months ago. She's a perfectionist, she kept coming back with her paints to put on 'the final touches'! But now it's done."

"It's magnificent," Salah agreed.

"Like living in a palace," said Nadia, grinning up at him. "Or is it?"

"It's like a page from a fairy tale!" Desi said, still gazing, and feeling a little as if she'd been put under an enchantment. "Who is the artist?"

"You may have heard of her. She is English, but she lives here in Western Barakat. Her name…"

"Oh, my God, is this an Anna Lamb? Of *course!*" Desi exclaimed. "She did one in London for Princess Esterhazy, and then everyone was after one! Fabulous, too, but not nearly as extensive as this."

Nadia stared at her for a moment, then smiled broadly.

"Oh my goodness! I *knew* I'd seen you before! You're *Desirée!* How amazing!"

"I didn't expect to be recognized so far from…home," Desi laughed. She was glad she had stopped before saying *civilisation.*

"We read *Vogue* in West Barakat, too! But what are you *doing* here? How do you come to know Salah?"

At that moment a dark, thin-faced man came into the room, closely followed by two servants carrying trays.

"Salah! Great to see you!" he cried, as the two men embraced. "What are you doing in Qabila?"

Salah turned. "Desi, this is my very good friend Ramiz."

Soon the four were seated on sofas around a low table, on which had been placed jugs of juice and water, and tall glasses.

"So why are you here? Just touring? Or is it a modelling assignment?" Nadia asked eagerly. "That would be exciting for us, to have Barakat used as a background."

"No, something much more interesting, as far as I'm concerned. I wouldn't spend days camping out in the desert for a shoot, let me tell you!" She paused and looked at Salah, wondering if his friends knew about his father's site.

"Camping out in the desert?" Nadia repeated in amazed tones. "In this heat?"

"Desi wants to see an archaeological dig in progress," Salah filled. "I'm taking her to Baba."

Ramiz's eyebrows went up. He exchanged a look with Salah, and then his eyelids drooped, masking his expression. The sound of a child's voice came from the next room, and for the first time Desi realized that one of the doorways under the painted arches was real.

"But I don't understand," Nadia said. "Why are you..?"

"You haven't seen Safiyah for a long time," Ramiz said to Salah, over her. "She misses you. You'll be surprised by how much she's grown. Tahir, too."

"Ayna Safiyah?" Salah called. *"Ayna walida jamilati?"*

The child's high shriek answered him, and then a little girl came tearing into the room and ran straight into his arms, followed by a woman carrying a baby.

"Aga Salah! Aga Salah!" the child cried.

Desi watched as Salah swung the shrieking child up into the air. His face was suddenly soft, his expression relaxed and warm. The face of the Salah she remembered.

He was not lost, the man she had loved. He was still there, underneath. If only she could reach him.

"Have you really been camping out in the desert at this time of year?" Nadia asked Desi against the background of the child's chatter. "What's Salah thinking of?"

"He did warn me, but I insisted. This is the only time I had to visit. The first night we stayed with nomads. Last night at Halimah's Rest."

Nadia frowned and shook her head. "Was the water clean enough to bathe in?"

"Call it a large puddle."

Nadia looked at her. "And then you drove all morning in the desert to get here? Salah must be crazy!"

"I haven't felt so grubby and sticky since I was five and my father took me for a day at the fair," Desi laughed.

"Desi," Nadia said hesitantly, "would you like to take a shower now? I am sure…"

"Oh, *could* I?"

So Nadia showed her to a bathroom, gave her towels and soap, and left her to indulge herself. Never had water been such bliss! She could have stayed under the cool flow for half an hour, but even here in Wadi Daud water must be a precious resource at this time of year. She restricted herself to five minutes.

She came out feeling human again, her newly washed hair twisted up on top of her head, her face cleansed, her skin breathing for the first time in two days. Heaven.

In the sitting room, meanwhile, Nadia took a protesting Safiyah away to get her lunch. Ramiz and Salah were left alone.

"Two days through the desert, via West Barakat, to get to your father's dig?" Ramiz asked softly.

"And we're only halfway there," Salah replied blandly. "It's a four-day trip. Nadia's not likely to mention where the dig is, is she?"

"Does she know? I don't, not with any accuracy. Subtle form of abduction, brother? She's very beautiful."

"Subtle form of interrogation. I want to know why she wants to see it."

"Ah." Ramiz pursed his lips. "Nadia recognized her. Super-model? She would have a lot of connections among the wealthy."

"Got it in one," Salah said.

"Could she be an innocent pawn?"

"No. I tried that one. She's hiding something."

Even as he spoke he wondered why he had brought Desi to this house, where the least slip would expose the truth of this expedition. Was he tired of the deception, had he somehow accepted that she was innocent, that last night had taught him her real reason for coming? Or had he merely fallen victim to her wiles in spite of his best intentions?

"The big mystery is, why has your father allowed it? Isn't the site completely shut down to outsiders?"

Salah nodded. "I advised him to refuse. His sense of justice wouldn't allow it. Desi's family in Canada hosted me very generously every summer for years when I was a kid learning English. He couldn't say no, even though we have to assume that whoever is behind it chose her for that very reason."

"So the desert is going to sweat the truth out of her?"

Salah nodded.

"And what else?" Ramiz asked.

Salah raised his eyebrows in surprise. "What do you mean?"

"There's more going on between you than just a spy story, Salah. The air catches fire every time you look at her. What else are you trying to sweat out of her?"

"I have an idea!" Nadia said.

After a delicious cold lunch of various kinds of salad, Salah and Desi were making moves to go.

"We have a very interesting site close to Qabila. Rock carvings, two thousand years old, Desi! If you stop the night with us, Salah, you can take Desi to see them this afternoon."

Desi glanced at Salah. It was tempting, the thought of a comfortable bed and cool sheets and a shower in the morning. But she was unsure what such an offer of hospitality meant.

Was this one of those moments when you were supposed to protest three times before accepting?

"Thank you, that's very kind," Desi said with a smile. "But it's such a long trip, and I am really eager to get there as soon as possible."

"But if you leave now, you will not get to the site till nearly sunset, maybe even after dark," Nadia said. "You may as well stay here and go tomorrow morning. Anyway, the road is safer in daylight."

A funny little silence fell over the table. Ramiz and Salah exchanged glances. Ramiz started to say something in Arabic, but Desi was already asking, "The road?"

"Yes, in the dark, you know, you can hit blown sand before you see it. Salah is a very good driver, but when sand grabs your wheels, it can be very uncomfortable."

"What road would that be?" Desi asked carefully.

Nadia smiled and waved vaguely with her hand. "The main road to Central Barakat, of course! I really don't understand why—"

"The dig is on the main road?"

"No, didn't you tell us once it's an hour or two off piste, Salah? But the secret is knowing where to turn off!"

"Really. A whole hour off the main road."

"*Shokran*, Nadia," Salah said. "But we'll go on. I prefer to do the last leg under cover of darkness. Harder to track us, if anyone is trying."

Fifteen

A few minutes later they were in the Land Cruiser again, heading down the valley.

"So, are we going to continue the circular tour for another two days?" Desi asked as soon as she was sure she could control herself. She had never been so angry in her life, mostly with herself. What a fool she had been! Dreaming dreams about a man who had already proven himself a selfish, faithless monster. A man, clearly, who was obsessed with honour because he had none.

"Desi…"

"Since your ancestors were faultless navigators, I assume the detour was planned. Did you mean me to get to the dig at all? Or was the great navigator planning to get lost and spend two weeks driving around in circles?"

"I told you I would not let you discover the way, Desi."

"Five days? Was that much bluff really necessary?"

"I have told you from the beginning that I am concerned about your motives. I thought after a few days in the desert you might tell me the truth."

"Your own particular brand of endurance test. Is that why you made love to me, too?" Her heart convulsed so that she felt sick. "To try and break me down? Hoping for a pillow confession?"

"I warned you there was no future for us."

She began to laugh unhappily. "Oh, you're as noble as they come! A true mountain warrior—what's the code you once told me?—generosity, hospitality, bravery in battle, and a good lover? Oh, yes, everything's there, except the generosity, the hospitality, and the bravery! What a cowardly way to fight a battle against a woman! God, you make me sick!"

A cloud of sand billowed up around the car as Salah slammed on the brakes and pulled off the road under a cluster of date palms. He turned to her, his black eyes blazing.

"What did you expect, Desi? You come to me with lies, but you want truth from me! I *have* to know why you came here, why you want to visit this place! My father could not say no to you, because I owe your family such a debt! Was it noble in you to take advantage of him in this way?"

"I am not taking advantage of him! Why do you suspect me? Why won't you believe me?" she shouted.

"Because you are lying to me. I know it. Do not deny it again, Desi, it makes you more of a liar!"

"How can you make love to me at night and then in the day believe I could be a cheat?"

"Because you are a cheat. You cannot be trusted. You are weak. This I learned ten years ago."

Her jaw fell open. Her eyes blazed outrage at him.

"*Me!* How dare you? I'm *sick* of this accusation, Salah! You're ten years older now, isn't it time you got a handle on what happened? All I did was love you, and if that's a sin, well,

I've paid for it in spades! You're the one who was weak! You're the one whose love didn't last past the first hurdle. Not me!"

"Do you pretend to rewrite history with me?" he demanded. "Do you pretend to forget what you did?"

"What *I* did? What did I do, exactly?"

"Why do you want to open this? You did not love me."

"That's what I said, all right. I was sixteen years old. You're the one who wrote the letter. You're the one who decided that we were not after all married in our hearts and therefore I wasn't pure enough for you!"

He narrowed his eyes at her. "Do you pretend still? You could not have gone to the bed of this old man if your love had been real. You know it."

"*Old man? Bed?* What are you talking about?"

"You know. The one they called your agent. Why do you pretend with me?"

"*Leo?*" she screeched incredulously. "*Three years later,* Salah! How long did you expect me to wait for you to see the light?"

"*What?*" he whispered.

But she was in full flood.

"Three years during which you never once tried to get in touch! What was I supposed to do? You rejected me in the most humiliating, shaming way possible! Was I supposed to beg? To promise to give up my too demeaning career? Grovel because I was weak and slept with you before we were bound in holy bloody matrimony?

"I waited and waited in the hopes that when you wrote it you were delirious or something, but no! Your self-righteousness was fully conscious! I don't know what the *hell* you think you had a right to expect…"

"What do you mean, three years later?" Salah finally found his voice, and it rasped like gravel against a screen.

"I was nearly nineteen before Leo's master plan came to fruition! Are you really presuming to blame me for that? You didn't want me, but I should remain virgin forever? What was it, some kind of sanctity test? No one else got near me for three years, Salah. Did *you* wait that long? I'd like to know."

His eyes were hollow with shock.

"He was your lover from the beginning! You went from me to him."

Her face convulsed with distaste. "No, he was *not!* I was sixteen, for God's sake! He was forty-two!"

"It wasn't true?" He was hoarse with horror.

"What?" Desi stared at him blankly. Then her eyes narrowed as suspicion took hold. "What do you mean? *What* wasn't true?"

"Sami sent me a magazine clipping. A picture of you with this old man. It said…"

Her head went back as if he had hit her. She stared at him, and for a moment they were frozen there, locked in mutual horror.

"You *believed* it?" She was open-mouthed with shock as the fact sank in. She stared, shook her head to try to clear it. "Is *that* why—?" she whispered. "How could you believe it?"

"Desi—"

"You, of all people! Did you really imagine that within a few weeks I could—? With you on a battlefield, for Christ's sake! You thought I had—" Suddenly feeling came rushing in to fill the blankness and her voice found its feet.

"You read something about me in a damned cheap-thrills sell-your-soul-for-a-dollar celebrity magazine, and you *believed it?*" She drew in a shuddering breath. "My God, it was bad enough when I thought…"

She didn't know where to look. She turned away from him, lifted her chin, breathing with her mouth open like a wounded animal, trying to get air. Chills rushed over her skin.

"Oh, God!" she moaned. "This can't be true! This is a nightmare…"

She closed her eyes. Opened them again. Fury flooded her.

"*That* was why you wrote that letter. Wasn't it? You—you faithless…*my* love not strong enough? How dare you talk to me as if— *You*! What was *your* love worth, if you could believe *that*? Without asking, without even accusing—you just read some innuendo in a photo caption, and believed it? Leaving me to the mercy of those vultures who were surrounding me! *Nothing!* I had *nothing* to defend myself with, if you didn't love me! Did you think of that?"

Salah looked like the survivor of an explosion. He stared at her, his eyes black with shock.

"No," he said.

"A caption under a picture! Not even a story!— I wanted to deny it, but Leo told me if we made a fuss it would only confirm it in people's minds. It was better to let it pass. Anyway, he said, this would make it easier for him to protect me from predatory men, the way he'd promised my father!

"And it did give me protection—of sorts! I was sixteen and pretty and not engaged to you. If Leo hadn't been in the background I'd never have had a moment's peace!"

With an upsurge of the sick bitterness that Leo's betrayal of trust had created, she added, "It didn't protect me from Leo himself, of course. He was the most predatory of all, but he could play the long game."

"*Ya Allah,*" Salah whispered. She had never seen his face the way it looked now.

"I hated it all. I'd never wanted the life, never! I always felt I was living some other girl's dream. But because it was so fantastic I somehow had to live it. I missed you so much! I wished and wished I'd never done that stupid ad. Then you'd never have said what you said, and we'd have been married and I wouldn't ever have met Leo. But I was so nervous. Over and over I started a letter to you, but each time I thought....

"And then you were wounded, and I knew none of that mattered, because I loved you and I would never love anyone else, and if you died, I died, too. I waited for you to answer my card, wondering if you would live, praying—God, how I begged for you to recover! And when I saw your letter lying there—!" Her eyes squeezed shut. "I nearly died from joy. I thought my heart was going to burst out of me and fly.

"Then I read it—and you know what? He may have waited three years before he physically climbed into my bed, but Leo got me in spirit the day I read your letter. I gave up that day. I gave up thinking what we had was special, that anything was special! I gave up what I'd believed about myself. I wasn't good enough for you, Salah. I'd loved you and wanted you too much, and because of that you thought I—"

She began to sob helplessly, feeling as if all the tears of a lifetime were waiting to be shed.

"I felt so cheap! I thought, well, if Salah can say such horrible, disgusting things…then it was all nothing. What I thought we had was nothing. It was never real. *You betrayed your honour.* It burned me like an iron. I'll remember that feeling till the day I die. I'd have given up that life in a minute, if you'd asked, but that letter told me it was more than being a model. I'd demeaned myself in your eyes by making love with you, too, that's what I believed. What we had wasn't beautiful at all, it was cheap and dirty. That was the end of everything."

He was silent, his eyes black, watching her, knowing without doubt that what she spoke was the truth.

"And now you tell me you wrote that filth because you believed—*how* could you believe it? And not even to ask me if it was true!" she cried, as the barriers gave way and all the hurt rushed into her throat, demanding release. "How could you think for a moment that I could go from you to him? I couldn't stand any other man touching me! Even three years after—the first time Leo…I was sick afterwards! I ran into the bathroom and threw up!"

She stopped and groped in her bag for tissues, then lifted her head and looked at him.

"It was bad enough when I thought you despised me for loving you or for being a model, but *this!* It's too much, Salah. This is unforgivable. You destroyed the most beautiful…what a cold, judgmental, untrusting bastard you were. Are. Well, I'm glad I know at last. And to think I've spent these few days with you regretting what we missed!" She added, in a self-disgust so total she could hardly breathe. "Imagining that we still had something that could…but we never had anything, did we? It was all a lie from the get-go. I'll never regret it again. I was lucky. I had a bloody lucky escape."

Then there was silence, broken only by the sound of her weeping.

Sixteen

Salah felt blank, the way one feels after a bullet has hit: the emptiness of waiting for the pain.

He sat staring into the past, as all the carefully constructed armour of ten years collapsed into rubble around him. He had destroyed the dream by his own hand. Feeling began to blast in, a storm of grief and self blame.

She was completely blameless. The fault had been entirely his from the beginning.

She was right. He had acted towards her without generosity, without honour, all the while pretending that the lack of honour was hers. Even the least degree of decency had required that he ask her for the truth before judging her. And even believing it true, shouldn't he have tried to understand the pressures of that new world? A man of forty-two, a girl of sixteen. What chance would she have stood? Why hadn't he seen it before? Why hadn't he judged differently when he got a little older?

He opened his mouth three times before he could speak.

"Desi. There isn't a word strong enough. What have I done? Desi, forgive me."

He put his hand out to her but, still weeping, she twisted away.

"*Forgive?* How can I forgive it?" she howled.

"Desi.*"* His voice sounded completely unlike him. "My God. What a fool I am. Worse than a fool. A devil."

She was sobbing inconsolably. "You said you loved me, you say now it was the biggest thing in your life—how could you think such a thing? How could you begin to believe it? Why didn't you at least give me a chance?"

He swallowed. Ten years. What could make amends for such a waste of life and love?

"Desi, I am sorry."

"Oh, great. Yes, that makes all the difference!"

The car was insufferably hot. Sweat was pouring off her, and she wound down the window and tried to catch her breath.

Salah started the engine. "We can't stay here."

He put the vehicle in gear and backed out onto the road again.

The sun was in the west, streaming into the car now from the front, now on the right, as the road curved and turned. It was burning hot, in spite of the air conditioning, and Desi felt sick with the brightness and the heat on her skin. For a few miles she twisted the sun visor this way and that, trying to block the rays, and then Salah pulled over again.

He got out, rummaged in the back for a moment, then came around to her side. Without a word he opened the door, lowered the window, tucked a cardboard window protector over the glass and rolled it back up. It covered the passenger window and a few inches of the windscreen, putting her in welcome shade.

When they were moving again, she said, "Thank you."

He nodded, swallowing, as if he could not trust himself to speak.

"You could have done that any time over the past three days, I suppose. But then, you had to sweat the truth out of me."

They drove in silence, passing other cars on the road, glimpsing herds of camels and goats at distant nomad camps in the bleak, bleak desert. After a while Salah turned off the road and headed out over the sand again.

She wondered how she could ever have imagined such a landscape magnificent. It was nothing but emptiness.

RU still in desert? RU seducing Salah??? What is happening? Plz call as soon as U get coverage.

Desi read this message from another life dimly, hardly taking it in. Reception was poor, and she shut off the phone without answering.

Another hour passed, and then they were winding through a curious forest of rocky outcrops and into a valley between high walls of rock. Green scrub clung to the rock face here and there, and in places the wheels sank into mud or splashed through a stagnant puddle. In other places a thin trickle gave promise that this was a river bed.

"In winter there are flash floods here," Salah said. "It is very dangerous." It was the first word that had passed between them for over an hour. "Two years ago all this area flooded for the first time in living memory. Even in the tribal traditions there was no history of such flooding."

"Ever the travel guide," she said.

Just before sunset the rock walls fell away and the vista opened up. The sky in the west was a brilliant fire of gold, with Mount Shir shining in white majesty over the growing shadows in the desert. In the distance she saw a collection of tents nestled beneath a stand of rock.

"My father's camp," said Salah.

It was as if a nomad encampment had entered a technology warp, and half its tents had been converted into air-conditioned caravans and trailers. All the modern equipment was nestled into the protective shadow between two large outcrops of black rock that jutted up from the desert floor. In front of them was ranged a nest of tents, half modern and half the low-slung nomadic type. And in front of that was the massive ancient site, where workers in straw hats toiled in rows, as if the nomads had taken to terrace farming. As they approached, an armed guard sitting on a rock peered at Salah's face for a moment and waved the vehicle on.

"I have to find out what arrangements have been made for us," Salah said, pulling up to park in the shade of a white trailer. "They are not expecting us yet. You can wait in the mess tent, Desi, or I can take you to my father."

It was far too hot to sit in the car, though that was what she would have preferred. Desi squeezed her eyes shut for a moment, struggling to find focus in her shell-shocked, blank state.

"There will be people in the mess tent?"

Salah nodded.

"Is there anywhere I can go and sit by myself?"

"Not till I find out which trailer they have arranged for you."

"Your father, then."

He led her to the long white caravan that served as the site office. Inside it was air-conditioned to a comparatively refreshing twenty-five degrees, nearly eighty Fahrenheit. Desi was desperately grateful to get out of the sun.

The archaeologist Dr. Khaled al Khouri was sitting at a desk inside. He was a solid, square-set man with grizzled grey hair, a face with deep lines furrowing his forehead and carved from his strongly cut nose to the corners of his mouth. When they entered he was engrossed in examining a dirt-impacted object with the sunburnt, intent young woman standing beside his chair.

Neither noticed them enter. They watched for a minute as the professor's strong, competent fingers prised off the dirt of millennia to fall unheeded on his papers, and revealed a goblet.

With caressing strokes that reminded Desi of Salah's hands on her body, he dusted down the little cup, turned it over, then held it still, gazing at the face of the bowl.

"You're right, Dina," he said at last. "Congratulations. Well done."

"Thank you, Dr. al Khouri."

"Leave it with me. I'll take it to Hormuz later."

As the young worker slipped through the door beside them, her eyes fell on Desi and she turned around to gasp in disbelief before continuing on her way. At the sound, the doctor lifted his head.

"Yes?" he said, and then, "Salah!"

"Desi, meet my Father," said Salah. "Father, this is Desirée Drummond—Desi."

"Desi! Hello!" Dr. al Khouri exclaimed, getting to his feet. He put out his hand, giving her the same focussed attention he had bestowed on the found object. The clasp of his hand was firm, reminding her of Salah's. The black eyes were friendly, but uncomfortably piercing.

"I am very happy to meet you at last. We have heard so much about you! It is kind of you to come to visit us."

He did not sound in the least like a man who suspected her of conspiring to steal priceless objects, and Desi flicked a glance at Salah.

"It's very kind of you to let me come," she said, and under the warm intensity of his gaze, she managed to find a smile.

Her hand had collected a certain amount of dirt during the handshake, and she absently dusted it down on her khaki shorts. Dr. al Khouri frowned, looking at his own hand.

"Too much dirt in this job!" he said, dusting his hands. "I must go out now and make my round before they down tools for the night. Perhaps you will like to come with me, Desi. You have come a long way, and I know you will be eager to see the site as soon as possible."

She nodded agreement. It was long past time to get away from Salah. Salah seemed to agree.

"I will check on the sleeping arrangements," he said. Their eyes caught for a moment, and she sent him a cold warning with her eyes. Then she saw that he did not need it: he had no more interest in their continuing to share a bed than she did. Well, he'd had his closure, of course, she reminded herself bitterly.

If only *she* could feel closure. But for Desi it was all still boiling up inside her, rage and heartbreak and a deep, abiding sense of betrayal.

A moment later she was out in the late sunshine, listening as Dr. al Khouri began to explain the site. He spoke as if she were the student she was pretending to be, and in spite of everything Desi began to be intrigued.

"Look at this," Khaled al Khouri told her, as they paused by a worker who was carefully excavating a massive slab embedded in the hardened soil, on which she could make out, faintly, an etched image. "This piece is our pride and joy."

Desi peered at it. "Is that a woman?"

"Not a woman," he said, with the air of a man used to correcting students. "All we can say with certainty at the moment is that this is a female figure. In fact, she is probably our goddess. We believe this lady might have been the tutelary deity of the whole civilisation."

She bent down to see more clearly. The figure showed the hint of a tiara in the intricately curled hair that fell down over her shoulders above wide-spaced breasts, a curving waist encircled by some kind of string or thong, broad hips and a prominent nest of pubic hair. One hand was at her side, the other held up in what might be a gesture of greeting, palm towards the viewer. She was standing on an animal that Desi could not distinguish.

Excitement bubbled up as she recognized her little goddess.

"Who is she?" she demanded.

"We think, the deity of this temple." The archaeologist waved his hand at the long shape marked out in the earth with stakes and string. "We don't know her name yet."

"Is she a fertility goddess? A love goddess?"

"We think so."

"Inanna?"

He lifted an eyebrow at her, in a gesture so like Salah her heart kicked a protest. "Possibly, but if so it's an unusual depiction of her that would be specific to this people, and she might have had another name. What made you think of her?"

Desi laughed. "She's the only ancient love goddess I know!" she confessed. "I bought a little statue from some nomads a couple of days ago. I think it's the same woman…female figure!"

Dr. al Khouri shook his head, sighing. "You bought her from nomads?"

"Yes, for twenty dirhams. She's in the truck."

"Then tomorrow you will show her to me. This, we suspect," he waved his arm to take in the entire site, "was her particular city. Perhaps the people came here on pilgrimages."

"The goddess of love was the chief god?" Desi asked, amazed.

"Yes, and such worship left its mark on later generations. In antiquity, Barakat has had many ruling women, and even after Islam, we often allowed queens to rule us. You have heard of the great Queen Halimah?"

"Yes."

"Her path was of course paved by the goddesses and queens of antiquity, who still exist in the psyche of Barakat."

"Oh!" Desi said in surprise.

"Your own little goddess probably came from this area, but not this particular site. The flooding brought many things to the surface all along the valley. We have seen evidence for at least two more large settlements not far away.

"That is why it is so critical to keep this secret for as long as possible. We can never hope to police every potential site in the valley, and if we lose too many of them...but we start with the largest, hoping that it is also the most important."

"Salah says looters aren't the worst threat, though," she remembered. He had said it only a day or two ago, Desi realized in distant surprise. She seemed to have lived a lifetime since then. Then she had felt alive, that was why it seemed so long ago.

"That is true."

The archaeologist guided her over a narrow bridge of land between two square holes, smiling and nodding at the diggers below, who were starting to call to each other about the happy prospect of downing tools and cold beer.

"Looters take what they find for their own enrichment. But the others, the fools who cannot bear to know that once the feminine was worshipped as fervently as the masculine is today, the idiots who must force the past to match their ideals as well as the present—they are a different kind of danger. They want to destroy the evidence.

"Whatever we find here, Desi, it is the heritage of the whole world. It is our collective history. These madmen— they want to forget that all of Mohammad's line comes through a woman. Fatima. Without his daughter, there would be no sharifs at all, no descendants of the prophet. But still they want to wipe the feminine out of the world."

"And you thought I might be helping these people?" she asked in quiet bitterness.

He stared at her. "Help them? What intelligent person would help such lunatics?"

"Salah said you suspected I wanted to come here because—"

"Oh!" he said, in a different tone. His eyes moved to her face. "My wife said that if we wanted Salah to be happy, I had to let you visit, in spite of Salah's objections. And I had to pretend to suspect your motives, too. I am only an archaeologist, I don't really understand these things. But you will know—is my son happy now?"

Her heart was suddenly beating in hard, heavy thuds. "How would I know?" Desi protested. "Isn't he going to marry Sami?"

He shrugged. "My wife says not."

Desi took a deep breath and sighed it out. *Promise me you'll tell Uncle Khaled only if you're absolutely certain he'll be all right with it,* Sami had said. And here was Sami's chance. This at least she could accomplish. This at least she could pull from the wreckage. No happiness for herself, that wasn't possible now, but...

She said, "Dr. al Khouri—"

"But you must call me Khaled!"

"Khaled, I have something to tell you, and something to ask you, from Sami."

"Ah, yes, my niece is your friend! My wife said. Let us sit here, then." He guided her to a bench beside a table under a canopy, where they had a view over the whole dig. "Now. What has to be said that my niece could not say to me herself?"

Desi stared out over the scene, watching long shadows move and dance as the workers moved out of the field and headed towards the tents.

"It's about…the marriage." Her voice grated on the word. "Sami asked me to tell you that she—doesn't want to marry Salah. She's already engaged to a man she loves, but her brothers wanted to choose her husband. It was they who chose Salah. She's told them she doesn't agree, but they…"

"Do you speak of Walid and Arif?" the scientist interrupted in amazement.

Desi nodded. "She asked me to beg you to overrule Walid and send your permission for her to marry the man she loves. Otherwise she's afraid Walid will do something…really stupid."

Khaled al Khouri's eyebrows went up as he inhaled all this, and when she stopped speaking he sighed explosively.

"Well, they are fools, these young nephews of mine! If they do not control themselves, they will soon be among the madmen who come to destroy history for the sake of their convictions. What is his name, Samiha's fiancé?"

"Farid Durrani al Muntazer. His family are originally from Bagestan, but he's Canadian."

"Madthe?" Khaled threw back his head and laughed a loud, boisterous laugh. "Well, they are worse than fools. They are ridiculous! This boy is a member of the royal family of Bagestan!"

Desi stared. "What?"

"This is one of the names the al Jawadi took decades ago when they went into exile. Why does he not tell them so? It is no secret anymore. They are on the throne now, as the world knows."

The Silk Revolution. Desi, like everyone else she knew, had been thrilled when handsome Sultan Ashraf had been restored to the throne of Bagestan. And Farid was related to him?

She smiled, and her heart lightened a little with happiness for her friend.

"I don't think Walid rejected him on his merits. It was the principle of the thing."

"Well, I will give her my formal permission, it is the only way with such young men as this. But I will also have something to say to them."

He stood and lifted a rope barrier for her.

"And now you have done your duty, Desi. Come and look at the Lady's temple before the sun goes."

Salah stood in the doorway of the mess tent, a cup of coffee in his hand, watching from a distance. The grace with which she moved up the long buried slope of that ancient temple where his distant ancestors had once worshipped love. In the shimmer of heat he seemed to see her through millennia. As if she belonged there, the high priestess of the religion of love.

Once he had worshipped at that shrine, had drunk from the honeyed chalice. Then with his own hand he had smashed it to fragments.

All the pieces of his life had come apart a few hours ago, and no new image had yet formed. He seemed to himself to be still staggering under the blow. All his landmarks were gone, blown down by the whirlwind of the horror of what he had done.

But the answer was here. He gazed at the lithe beauty of her as she talked earnestly to his father. She lifted her arm to point into the distance, and a last ray of the setting sun caught her suddenly, haloing her figure with flames of red gold, imprinting the shape on his heart, where it matched some shape already there....

The answer would be found here.

"Everyone eats in the food tent," Salah told her a little later, leading her across the moonshadowed desert towards the trailer where she would sleep. "Supper will be ready in half an hour. Or someone can bring you a tray here."

Desi heaved a breath. Everything was suddenly catching up with her, and she knew she couldn't sit through a meal with the bunch of cheerful, enthusiastic volunteers she had seen in her tour of the site, especially as it seemed all the starstruck girls were going to want her autograph. She would feel stronger in the morning. Right now she felt she would burst if the least demand were made on her. She desperately needed to be by herself.

"I'm not hungry. If I can have a glass of water I'll go to bed now."

"There's water in the trailer. Desi, I—"

"No," she said, flinging up a hand, her voice cracking with emotion. "Please. There's nothing to say."

"There is everything to say," Salah said. "Do you think we can leave it where it is?"

She couldn't take any more. Not tonight. Not ever. "I'll say good night, Salah."

But his hand closed on her arm, heat burning through her skin to war with the coldness in her heart.

"Walk with me," he said. *"Deezee!"*

Even now, even after what she had learned, his voice roughing up her name had power over her, like a cat's tongue on a sensitive spot. The knowledge filled her with distant fury. That nickname in his mouth was like blasphemy now. Bitter hurt welled up in her, choking her so that she could not speak to resist.

"Come with me."

And she turned and went with him out beyond the cluster of caravans and trailers, into the empty desert.

A full moon was climbing up the sky. The giant rocks threw heavy black shadows onto the sand, making a landscape unlike anything she had ever seen before, strange and other-worldly.

"Desi, I was blind. Blind and a fool."

She closed her eyes as a sense of waste and devastation flooded her. She shook her head.

"Too late," she choked. "Too little, too late."

"Don't say it!" he commanded. "It can't be too late, Desi. I won't let it be too late! We are still young, we have so much life in front of us."

"Are you young? I'm old. I feel a hundred years old. I'm tired and life has passed me by. And I don't want to talk about this. Is that all you wanted to say?"

He stopped and turned to face her. Moonlight carved his face like rock.

"What are you saying? Do you think we can just walk away from this? You loved me once. Love is still possible. That I know. When we make love, you tell me so in everything but words. Desi, I—"

She felt exhausted, bruised. "I think our watches must be out of sync, Salah." She glanced down at her wrist in the milky gloom. "Yeah, by, let's see—about ten years."

"A mistake destroyed those ten years," he insisted. "A stupid, ignorant mistake. And if we don't mend it now, it will destroy the rest of our lives. We have to find our way through this."

"The only mistake that would destroy the rest of my life would be to listen to you."

"You know it is not true. You would not be so hurt now if you did not… Please. Let us not go on in this terrible error. Look into your heart, Desi, and hear me."

Like a wounded animal goaded beyond its endurance, she rounded on him.

"Look! You wanted closure, am I right? That's what you wanted! Now you've had closure. You're going to get married, I think you said. Well, off you go, and good luck to you!"

"Do you think I can marry Sami now?" he almost shouted.

"But it doesn't matter who you marry, does it?" she

reminded him harshly. "What happened to 'the best love comes after marriage'?"

"How can I marry another woman *now* in the hopes of learning to love her?"

"I have no idea. But then I never understood the principle in the first place."

"Desi, I made a mistake. That mistake has ruined our lives for ten years."

"You're a powerful Cup Companion who lives in a palace. I don't wake up for less than ten thousand dollars. I don't think we can call this ruination."

"You speak of the world. I speak of the heart."

"Do you?" Desi gave vent to a snort of bitter laughter. "That's a good one!"

"Desi, you have to forgive me! Forgive me and let's leave this in the past, where it belongs. Stay with me tonight, Desi. Let me love you again. Love me. Let us find our hearts' truth together."

Panic choked her. Her heart was kicking like a drum, and there were too many words in her throat.

"Love you? Love the man who only yesterday believed I was conspiring to destroy his country's history and culture? The man who for ten years judged me by a piece of trash magazine gossip and never bothered to find out the truth? Gosh, I wonder what I should say to this? Will a simple *no* do, or should I point out that I wouldn't touch you again if you were the last man standing after Armageddon?"

"Desi—"

"And that if you so much as touch me, I will blast you down so hard Armageddon will look like a tea party. Please, I can't take any more of this! If you've said what you had to say, I want to go back."

He gazed down into her anguished face in the moonlight, lifted his head for a moment, breathed deeply, then turned their steps. Their moonshadow moved ahead of them now, disguising the path, making it harder to find their footing. Desi felt seasick, as if she'd had too much sun.

"Can you understand that I was suspicious of your motives because I didn't trust my own?" Salah asked quietly.

"What the hell's that supposed to mean?"

"You know what I mean. You said it yourself. When I said I only wanted closure I was lying to myself. When I accused you of lying I was looking in a mirror."

"I'm thrilled for you if you see it, however belatedly."

"Desi," he commanded.

She turned her head to look at him, her jaw tight. His shadowed eyes glinted moonlight at her.

"I told you once that we were already married, in our hearts. That we would be married forever. Do you remember?"

"*I* never forgot."

"Once I forgot it, Desi. I am sorry. Please don't—"

"You forgot it a lot more than once."

"A man may not live up to the truth, but the truth is no less true."

"Whatever that means."

"We are married in our hearts. We always were."

"Didn't we get a divorce?" she asked brightly. "I think I remember that."

"We can fix that mistake now. Think how many more years there are ahead of us. What if we live to eighty? Ten years of misunderstanding will be nothing."

They had reached her trailer now. Desi went up the step, then turned and faced him, her hand on the latch.

"The last ten years will never be nothing to me," she said stonily. "But you will, Salah. You are. Nothing to me. Good night."

She went in and closed the door.

* * *

Sleep would not come. She lay like one fatally wounded, re-examining her life and her ten lost years. The shame she'd carried for so long after reading Salah's letter. That miserable year-long affair with a man almost as old as her father. And afterwards, feeling so permanently degraded it was as if all sexual life in her died. Until Salah himself had brought her to life again.

Leo could never have succeeded, of course, had she not felt so despised. She remembered her stunned shock at the gross betrayal of trust after three years of acting like a father to her. There was no one she'd trusted more.

"Oh, come off it!" he'd said impatiently. "Don't try and tell me you haven't been expecting this! Why do you think I've invested so much time and money in you, Desi? Building a career you would never have had without me. You're not quite as fabulous as we've got them saying, you know! Without me you'd still be posing in cheap anoraks for catalogues in the backwoods."

She'd accepted it, too stunned to resist either the judgement or his advances. She accepted his marriage proposal, too. That ten months of being Leo Patrick's fiancée had been three hundred days of humiliation, until she had found the courage to break with him completely, find her feet and a new agent.

Salah's judgement of her had become a self-fulfilling prophecy.

If Salah had trusted her, that awful year could not have taken place. Her life would now be something else entirely. The possibility of happiness would not seem so distant.

Was it only yesterday she had realized she had never stopped loving him? Where was that feeling now? He had betrayed the past, and it ran like a seam all through her life.

And now he wanted her again, he said. Not just physically, this time: no, now he wanted her love.

But he'd killed that. A love that had survived, buried but intact, for ten long desperate years, had finally been put out of its misery. *You killed it with your own hand,* Desi told Salah silently. *And all things considered, I should be grateful. One day I will be. When I've recovered, I'll be glad.*

Then she turned to bury her tears in her pillow.

Seventeen

"We knew there was a VIP coming," the girl gushed happily. "We thought it would be the French Culture Minister or somebody like that. I mean, who would have thought it would be *Desi?*"

The noon sun painted the world a painful, bright white outside the open-fronted mess tent, where she was sitting with Salah and his father and a couple of the dig supervisors over lunch. She had awoken with a headache and stayed in the trailer to miss breakfast. Then she had done the rounds with Salah's father again, keeping all possibility of conversation with Salah at bay.

But she had to face Salah sometime, so when Khaled had mentioned lunch, Desi hadn't protested. She and Salah still had not spoken, but in the bustle no one seemed to notice.

She glanced at him once, and that once was enough to tell her she'd had no need for evasive tactics: the window of opportunity was closed. Salah was back in control. The anguish of last night was gone, his face today was shuttered stone. He was the Salah she had met at the airport once more—harsh, forbidding, a man who was nobody's fool.

That was good, of course. She was glad. Now all she wanted to do was get away from him as soon as possible.

Desi smiled and signed her autograph in the thick, grubby notebook labelled FIELD NOTES for the young volunteer, who had finally summoned the courage to approach the table and speak to her. Others were watching from a distance and it was clear they would join their friend in another minute.

"So are you going to be having pictures taken here? Is it, like, a modelling shoot?" the girl asked.

Suddenly there was the sound of a vehicle engine approaching, and everyone sat up with ears pricked as it came to a stop outside the tent.

"Are we expecting someone?" Dr. al Khouri asked. Everyone at the table shook their head. "I hope the guards were awake," the archaeologist said grimly.

A car door slammed, and a moment later a woman's figure appeared in the tent opening, features indistinguishable against the light. She paused briefly in the entrance, swept a look around the tables, then headed firmly towards the table where they were sitting. Desi saw an elegant woman with an aristocratic face and alert black eyes.

"Mother?" exploded Salah in disapproving amazement. "What are you doing here in such heat?"

"I came to meet Desi, of course," said Arwa al Khouri.

"This is my husband's home on site," Salah's mother said a little later, as they entered a cool, if rather cramped and untidy trailer. "I am not often here, because the heat is bad for my health.

"So. You will call me Arwa, yes?" she said, shifting a pile of papers from the sofa to the floor so that they could sit down. "I feel that I have known you a very long time already! It is only bad luck, after all, that we have not met long ago."

"You speak such good English!" Desi said brightly, nervously steering the conversational boat towards the shallows.

Arwa was an elegant, aristocratic woman whose black hair had been cut probably, Desi guessed, in Paris, where she doubtless also bought her clothes. Her skin was firm and clear without any sign of surgical or chemical assistance, and Desi thought she must be about fifteen years younger than her husband. Wearing a smart pink linen tunic and trousers, she made Desi feel grubby and underdressed in her khaki shorts, t-shirt and the loose khaki shirt.

"Not so good. But I am glad that you and I can talk without an interpreter. I am so glad to meet you at last, Desi! Because I go every year to Paris for the shows, I have seen you several times on the catwalk. And I so wanted to meet you! Each time I thought, if I just send a note…but always I lacked courage."

Desi had heard this kind of thing many times, but from a woman like Arwa al Khouri it surprised her.

"Why did you want to meet me?"

"Because you were the woman who had my son's heart, and there was trouble between you," Arwa said simply. "I am so glad to meet you at last, Desi." She reached out to pat Desi's arm. "So glad you have finally come."

Desi stared, discovered that her mouth was hanging open, closed it, felt it open again of its own volition.

"What—what are you talking about?" she asked stupidly.

"Now, you won't worry that I am his mother," said Arwa. "You will tell me everything, yes? Because I look into your eyes, Desi, and I think I see that you do love my son. As of course he loves you."

Desi shook her head, because suddenly she couldn't trust herself to speak. She thought of the stony face that had greeted her at lunch today. Whatever he had briefly imagined yesterday, she knew Salah was impervious to love. For one treacherous moment Desi regretted last night's outburst. If she had let him speak when he wanted to…

No. She'd been right before. She'd had a lucky escape ten years ago.

"Tell me," Arwa invited.

A moment ago she had imagined she was in control of herself. Now, suddenly, Desi was horrified to find herself close to tears. She gulped and shook her head, but it was all too recent, she couldn't contain her grief. She had never told anyone the whole story, not even Sami knew. But now the words began to spill out, as if with a will of their own, until she had unloaded everything. The letter that had destroyed her ten years ago, the discovery of why he had written it. His baseless accusations about her motive for the visit.

"Never once did he take me on trust! Never once in ten years! I don't call that love!" Desi finished at last.

Salah's mother did not speak till Desi had stopped talking. Then she sat shaking her head.

"And in this way he has nearly destroyed himself, and you, too," she said. "Men can be such fools when they love too much. But I think I understand my son. I see how it happened."

"So do I," Desi said, hiccuping. "It's no mystery, is it?"

"He was very young and our two cultures are so different. Ten years ago such advertising pictures of women were rare here in Barakat, Desi. Even now they do not appear often. So to see you in such a way was a shock for Salah. Of course he did not react well, but he regretted it almost immediately, you say. He did beg forgiveness. And then you, from your own cultural distance, mistrusted Salah in return."

"*I* mistrusted *him?*"

Arwa smiled. "But what else was it, when you feared—on the evidence of one jealous outburst!—that he was like those Kaljuk fools who punish women for their own inadequacies? He believed you were being sexually exploited, but you feared he could be a madman."

Desi went still as it sank in. She had blamed Salah for not trusting her, but she had never recognized her own fears as mistrust of him. On what evidence had she judged him? One argument, and he was sharing a mindset with the lowest of the low.

"When he returned from his visit with your family that year, I knew he was very unhappy," his mother recalled softly. "But he would not talk to us. And the next thing we knew, instead of going to university as he should, he enlisted in Prince Omar's troop of Cup Companions and went off to fight the Kaljuk War.

"And a few months later, he was wounded. The bullet missed killing him by a centimetre and he fell down the side of the mountain and suffered more injuries. The first time I saw him…."

She put her hand up and massaged between her eyes as if the memory still haunted her. After a moment she went on.

"And you tell me it was at this time—just when he was at his weakest, when he was in terrible pain and fear and had only his own determination to tell him he would recover—that he read something that told him you had gone to another man. And he believed it."

Arwa paused, but Desi's throat was too dry for speech.

"He should have questioned it, of course. But in the Barakat Emirates, again, we do not have such magazines as these. How could he know that they publish rumour as fact?"

Desi felt as though all her certainties were so many logs in the rapids and she could no longer keep her balance on them.

"Did he tell you about this? Is that how you know?" she asked.

"No," Arwa said firmly. "How I wish he had! We did not know at all what had happened, except that he loved you and you had broken his heart."

"If he didn't tell you, how could you know I broke his heart?"

Arwa smiled sadly.

"Desi, ten years ago, I sat beside my son's bed when we did not know if he would live or die. Every day and every night he called your name. He begged your forgiveness. He told you he loved you.

"We knew who Desi was—the young sister of his friend Harry. We knew you were only fifteen or sixteen. We discussed it many times during those terrible days, my husband and I, whether to get in touch and ask you to come to him." She shrugged. "We were afraid, and we did nothing."

"I wanted to come to him," Desi whispered. "But my agent said…"

But she had known. If only she had listened to her heart, and walked away from Leo and his "important bookings"! Then there would have been no room for misunderstanding. Why had she been so weak?

Salah was right—it was Leo who had come between them. He had not come to her bed then, but he had taken possession of her as surely as a lover.

Arwa sighed. "After these few weeks there was a big improvement. We brought him home. He was happier then, he was recovering. And then one day I went into his room, and my son was gone. Someone lay in the bed who looked like him, but it was not Salah. It was as if his inner self had died. I never learned what had happened, Desi—but I think perhaps today I know.

"And for ten years I never saw my son himself again—until the day his father told him that Desirée Drummond was coming to visit the dig. In that moment, I tell you, a mask was ripped away, and I saw that inside the stranger we had known for ten years was still my son Salah, and that you had the power to bring him back.

"Today I see that my son is alive again. His heart is breaking again, but at least it speaks to him. Salah recovered physically a long time ago, Desi, but today, for the first time since that terrible war, his spirit is alive.

"You ask how I know he loves you. That is how I know. Your presence has touched him as no one else can do. He doubted your love at a time when he was ill and vulnerable, it is true. And that weakness has led to misery for both of you. But if you love him—and why else have you come here?— you must find a way to forgive him, don't you think?"

Desirée gazed at her, torn between hope and grief. Was it true? Did his mother see something she herself had not seen behind the cold mask of Salah's face today? Could it be un- happiness, not coldness, that had turned his face to stone?

Her heart was being torn to ribbons, but one thing at last was clear. She could admit it now. She loved him. She did love him. And if he loved her...

What shook her most was the knowledge that the change she had seen in Salah, the thing that had turned him into the harsh, closed man she had hardly recognized at the airport was—herself. His conviction that she did not love him.

That was so much to absorb that she wasn't sure it would ever sink in completely.

Eighteen

"Will you walk with me, Desi?" Salah said.

It was sunset, and the air was cooling quickly. She looked up into his face and nodded once, then looked away again.

The setting sun coloured the great outcrops of rock all across the desert deep pink and gold as they walked out into the deserted ancient city. It was easy to feel the pull of another age, feel that she had almost slipped in among the people who had worshipped the feminine principle.

Easy to feel the female power that was deep in the fabric of the temple under her feet burn up through her.

They climbed the brick steps of the exposed remains of the great temple, and as her feet pressed into the ancient brick, built by hands dead five thousand years, Desi was flooded by a sense of otherness, a different way of being. A feeling of uninhibited joy embedded in the brick seemed to lift a burden from her.

She yearned to know these people. Who were they? How did they worship the divine they revered as Goddess?

Desi said, "I asked your father this afternoon—he's agreed to take me on as a volunteer next season. There's something about this place. I want to be in on the discoveries. I want to know about her."

He thought of how it would be, to know she was here, day after day, if she were not his, and his heart clenched, but he could not protest.

Salah said softly, "You are the representative of the Goddess on earth, Desi, do you know that? She has to come to the world in disguise now, to hide her true face in a masculine world. So she manifests as a supermodel or a cinema star. This is the secret way the world now worships the feminine.

"I was wrong, ten years ago. It is not demeaning. They try to demean it, but in a woman like you, this female power comes forth unsullied.

"When they admire you and yearn for you, Desi, it is my father's lost Goddess that they seek. You keep her alive in the world. If she were not always alive in the world, the world would have been destroyed by human stupidity long ago. I see that now."

There was no answer she could find to that. But he did not seem to expect one. They stood and watched in silence until the sun had disappeared and stars spangled the blackness.

"Listen, Desi," he began urgently, as night settled around them, shrouding the sound of voices from the tents. "Please listen. I want to tell you how it was with me. Maybe if I tell you, your hurt will be less. I want to tell you."

"I'm listening, Salah," she said quietly.

"In the hospital you were there with me day and night. You were so much with me that finally it was as if I was thinking your thoughts. Then I learned with certainty that you did love me. It was fear that had made you deny it. And for the first time, Desi, I understood those fears. I thought of the savages in Kaljukistan and understood why my outburst had made you think I was like them. You knew so little of me, of my people.

"But I was not like them. I never could be. I never admired such men, openly or secretly."

"I know you couldn't," she whispered.

"And I knew, I *knew,* that our love could overcome everything. My jealous stupidity, your fear. We loved each other so much, we had touched a deep well that most people never reach. I knew it would be forever. I knew I had to get better, go and find you, and make it happen.

"From that moment, I began to recover. They brought me home.

"I was writing you a letter. I could write only a little at a time, but I was filled with confidence. In the letter I told you what I had learned, what I knew. I asked you to come.

"Then, before it was finished—so close, it was almost done! What demon interfered at that moment, Desi?—they brought me some mail, letters that had been following me for weeks, from home to Parvan, to the hospital and back home again.

"There was a letter from Sami, weeks old. From before I was wounded."

Sami, excited by her friend's success, had enclosed pictures cut from a magazine of Desi in her new life. He looked at the pictures and into another world. Desi was a different woman—polished, glossy, her hair perfection, diamonds at her ears and around her neck, her dress tight and short, her heels impossibly high. But worst of all was the smile, a smile he didn't recognize. It was wide, but it didn't reach her eyes.

"I went cold, Desi. I started to shiver. My heart stopped

with the fear that my feeling was wrong, that it was too late for us. The longer I looked at the pictures the more I was afraid. My certainty crumbled. I thought, *she belongs to this other world now, she will laugh at my letter.*"

But still, he would have sent the letter. It was better to be laughed at than not to try.

The last photo showed her with a man with a fake tan and a stitched-on smile, hovering over her with predatory possessiveness. Underneath, there was a caption. He still remembered it word for word.

"*'Leo J. Patrick with his latest discovery, the stunning Desirée. He's calling her the find of his life. Reliable sources suggest he's not talking strictly business. Apparently it's a May-December romance.'*"

"I didn't understand *May-December* until I asked. But I understood *romance*." He closed his eyes at the memory, opened them again. "It was worse than death, Desi. The pain carried all my confidence, all my security away."

Two days later her own card had come. It was stilted and awkward, and made nothing clear. *With love, your friend, Desi,* it said.

"I had lost all my insight into your thoughts. I thought this was your way of saying we should be friends. But I could not be friends with you, Desi. I wanted to be your lover, your husband, not friend while another man was your lover."

He stood gazing out over the purple-shadowed desert.

"I don't know what happened to me. I don't know why I never questioned the truth of it. Fool that I was. Did my illness make me crazy? I don't know. I only know the pain was much worse than my physical wounds, and that I wished the bullet had killed me.

"I wrote that letter. When it was sent I regretted it. And then I didn't again."

Desi's heart was kicking in her breast, pumping hope and fear in equal measure through her system. She couldn't speak, couldn't look at him. She bent her head, listening with every cell of her being.

When he recovered, he was to go to university abroad. His parents suggested Canada, but Salah rejected the idea. He chose London instead. But London was not the place to escape from thoughts of Desi. Her picture was in every magazine and newspaper, her name in too many gossip columns. One day he read that she was engaged to Leo J. Patrick, a year later he heard of the breakup on television.

Even then a part of him had wanted to go to her, fight for another chance. But he had struggled against the desire as foolish weakness, and won.

"I was a fool. So much worse than a fool. I killed it with my own hand. And now you hate me, and how can I complain? It was not you, Desi. I see it now. It is myself I have been angry with all these years. I was the one who killed our love."

It was not true, of course. He had been living a lie. Nothing had killed his love. He had loved her from that day to this, without ceasing for the space of a breath.

"Salah, I…" but she could not put anything into words.

"If you come to my country, Desi," he said, "to work with my father, you must understand that I will be here, too."

"Yes?"

"And when I see you, Desi, I will try to make you love me again. No more now than ten years ago am I capable of being your friend."

"No?" she whispered.

"Desi, I love you," said Salah. "Tell me I'm not too late. Tell me there is a way to make you love me again."

The moon was rising, fat and full-bellied, lighting the sand with her own particular glow. Her heart climbed with it, up among the stars. Her eyes burned with unshed tears.

Below them in the compound, lamps were lit. The table in the dining tent was being laid with food. Men and women came out of their tents, refreshed by the cool night air and the shower each was entitled to at the end of the working day. Their voices rang back and forth in the darkness, cheerful and ordinary, belying her feeling of mysterious communion with the distant ancestresses who had built this place.

He waited, gazing at the shadows below, listening to her soft breath, closer than his own heart, waiting for her answer.

"It wasn't all your fault, Salah," she began softly, struggling for calm against the wild fluttering of her heart. "For a long time I thought so. But I'm as much to blame as you are. So let's not talk about fault anymore. I'm tired of guilt and blame."

He turned her to him, and gazed into her face. Moonlight both revealed and cloaked it in mystery, and she was as haunting and elusive as the great feminine power that had once been worshipped here. He would spend the rest of his life in pursuit of her mystery.

"Desi?" he said.

She said, learning it even as she spoke, "I've been realizing something. It was never my own dream, to be a model. All the girls at school were so thrilled when I was 'discovered', when I started getting jobs, they all fantasized about supermodel stardom, and it was great, but…it just had never been my particular dream.

"When we fell in love, you and I, that was the dream I recognized. And I see now that I could have changed everything that night, if I'd only admitted it to myself, if I'd said to you—it doesn't matter about that ad because we're going to get married and it won't happen again…none of it would have happened. But I was caught in someone else's dream."

He said, "I attacked you. How could you answer but by resisting the attack? It is human nature."

"You didn't kill my love, Salah," Desi breathed. "Sometimes I wished you had. It hurt so much. But I know now I never stopped loving you. I was as wrong and weak as you were. But we were so young, and it was so powerful. I suppose we ought to be grateful it didn't kill us both outright."

"Desi," he said, in a voice suffocated with hope, "I love you. I will love you forever."

"I love you, too, Salah. Forever. I know it now."

Then his arms wrapped her in a fierce embrace, pulling her tight against him as he gazed hungrily down into her face. "Say you will marry me!" he demanded. "Tell me!"

Moonlight spangled the tears on her lashes, but she smiled at him.

"How can I say no? After all, we're already married in our hearts, aren't we?"

"Yes, beloved," he said, as his lips touched and tasted hers. "We are already married in our hearts."

Epilogue

"Mission accomplished," Desi said into the phone.

They had driven back to the palace in the morning, and Desi had called Sami to tell her the news.

"Oh, you *magician!*" Sami cried. "Thank you, thank you! How did you manage it, Des? Did you—what did you do?"

"It was easy. I just had to agree to marry Salah in your place. No sacrifice too great."

Sami screeched.

"I knew it! I knew he still loved you! I knew if he just saw you he'd… I've always thought it wasn't over for you two! That's wonderful, Des! Do you love him? Have you loved each other all this time?

"Yes, and yes."

"I am over the moon for you! And what about Farid?" Sami demanded anxiously. "Did you…did you get a chance to ask Uncle Khaled?"

"He said something kind of interesting. Did you know your fiancé is related to the Sultan of Bagestan?"

"My *fiancé?*" Sami caught it instantly. "Has Uncle Khaled actually given his consent?"

"He's going to tear a strip off Arif and Walid, too, as I understand it."

"Oh, that's wonderful, Des! Oh, thank you, thank you!" her voice caught, and for a moment she couldn't speak. "I am so—but I knew it would all come right, if you would just— I knew you and Salah would…"

"Sam! Are you telling me you were *counting on—*"

"*Allah,* I'm delirious with relief!" Sam sniffed loudly and laughed on a sob. "Are you as happy as I am, Des? You sound…wait a minute! *Des!* What did you just say about Farid? He's related to *whom?*"

He held the wife of his heart in his arms, and looked into her eyes, and nothing came between them. No shadow of the past, no fear for the future clouded the perfect communion of that gaze.

Her hair lay spread over his arm and the pillow, where the lamplight kissed it tenderly. She smiled up into his face, and he marvelled at the trusting openness, the vulnerable offering of the deepest parts of the soul he saw in her eyes, not realizing that the look was reflected in his own gaze.

"Beloved," he murmured, and bent to brush her perfect lips with a kiss. Gently, sweetly, as tenderly as moonlight, his lips caressed her mouth, her cheek, her temple, her throat.

Melting followed every lightest touch, and she smiled and heaved a long, slow breath. She wrapped an arm around him, drawing him close, and pressed her own mouth to his cheek, his strong throat, his mouth.

"I love you so much, Salah," she whispered. "Please love me."

His body stirred and pushed against her, and she melted deep inside, in anticipation of his homecoming. His hunger tightened his arms around her, his mouth grew more demanding, drinking deep of the delights of those soft lips, that eager tongue.

He began to stroke her, but she did not want delay. She wanted union. She pressed up against him, slipped impatiently under his body.

"Love me," she said again. "I want to feel you inside."

He could not resist such a command. Was this how the Goddess had treated her worshippers? Demanding her pleasure of them?

He would always be a worshipper at this shrine.

He slipped into the cradle of her hips, lifted himself while she fitted up against him, and hungrily pushed home. They gasped together as the blow pushed pleasure into every cell, and lay for a moment of surprise, looking into each other's wide eyes.

In the moonlight she was both mysterious and known, both his and the other, the unknowable. He realized he must make her his, all his, and his body instinctively rose and pressed home again, to repeat that burst of joy, for this, he knew, was the way to own the lady. Her weakness for pleasure would always make her his.

He drew away and then home again, over and over, listening to the rhythm of her cries, guided by her hands, her mouth, her eyes, the hiss of breath between her teeth.

His own pleasure was his at any time, such power she had over him. But it was his delight to withhold it while he pushed her closer and closer to the source of the lady's mysterious power.

Melting pleasure flooded through her with each thrust of his body, and stored itself up in her cells, waiting for release. She lifted her body in response to the rhythm that had been created before the world. This was the rhythm of the birth of worlds, she thought dimly, this was how it happened—this endlessly repeated, endlessly building heat and joy, the sending of light into her heart, her muscles, her cells, her atoms. The pushing and pushing against the barrier that divided body from spirit, soul from soul, the barrier that only joy could defeat.

The pleasure built up in her till there was no room for any more, and still it built, overflowing from her cells into the world, till they were surrounded by an aura of sweetness and light and warmth that was all and everything, a warmed honey that glowed with its own light, an all-embracing delight-in-waiting.

And still he pushed, and pushed more, till she was sobbing with her inability to contain the pleasure, and then, suddenly, there was an explosion of heat and light, of love and joy, of delight and honey, and the wild need to be both self and other.

Pleasure blasted its way through them, and then what they hungered for was within their grasp, and they reached for it together, clasped it and brought it down to their bed, and held it for that brief, endless moment that is all that is allowed to mortals.

Afterwards they lay in each other's embrace, talking and silent, loving and still.

"Prince Omar has asked you to go and live abroad?" she asked. "Why?"

"He wants me to set up as an unscrupulous collector, and let it be known I'm interested in Barakati antiquities, whatever their provenance."

"With the goal of?"

"We hope it will allow us to trace the lines of supply right back to source. With luck we might bring down the whole chain."

"And what happens when you've finished the job? Salah, you won't expect me to live in Barakat full time?" she asked.

His arm tightened around her.

"I know your career means you have to be in Paris and London. We'll find a way, Desi."

"Only a few more years," she admitted. "I'm very tired of the life. But I've been thinking for a while that I'd like to get a place on one of the islands and spend a few months of the year there. Not too far from my parents. Would you go for that?"

"I always liked the island," he said. "Summers there were always more pleasant than here in the desert."

She grinned. "I don't think I ever understood quite how much until these past few days."

"And what about your work with my father?"

"Yes, I'm looking forward to that! I'm definitely going to see if I can fit in some part time study this year. Sami says everything gets taped now and you can download lectures. So it should be doable."

"I'm glad you have found a new career with my father, Desi. And I have another apology to make. How many times did I accuse you of lying? I was so sure I knew you!"

"Yes," she said curiously, tilting her head to look up at him. "What made you so sure?"

He smiled and lifted a strand of her hair to tickle his mouth.

"Even when we were children and you came in to tell the rest of us stories, or when you said something to challenge me—I always knew when you'd made it up, remember?"

"Oh!" Desi cried, remembering. "*Yes,* how infuriating that was! Harry would have swallowed anything, but for you! How did you always *know?*"

"Well, I will tell you, though perhaps it sounds impossible in the cold light of reason. The colour of your eyes changed. When you had something to hide, your eyes were grey.

"I was already suspicious of your motives before you

came. I told my father so, and he agreed it was suspicious. But when you were telling me your reasons for coming here, and your eyes went grey…then I was sure you were lying."

"Ahhh," Desi said. "No one's ever told me that before."

"I could think of only two reasons for you to be here. I told my father you were the tool of thieves—I told myself that that was why I had to be your guide. But I couldn't suppress the hope—not that I saw the feeling as hope then!—that you had really come here for…"

"For you? You secretly wanted me to say, *you can't marry Sami because I still love you?*"

"Things might have proceeded more quickly if you had."

"Sami made me swear a terrible oath that I wouldn't tell you the truth. Otherwise I'd have cracked a dozen different times."

It took a moment for that to filter in. He propped himself up on one elbow and stared down at her. In the lamplight clear turquoise eyes smiled up at him.

"What? What truth?"

"You were right, Salah. I *was* lying to you. Not for my own ends, though—well, not consciously. I came here because of Sami."

She felt his surprise. "Sami?"

"I guess your father never had the chance to tell you. Sami has a fiancé already. She doesn't want to marry you. Please don't break your heart. She asked me to—well, to try and… sidetrack you. And to try to get your father's permission for her to marry Farid instead of you."

"But this is crazy! It was they who made—"

"It wasn't Sam's doing, though. Her brothers have forced her into a lot of observant practice over the past few years."

He wouldn't rest till he had the whole story out of her. Then he lay back laughing.

"You were supposed to compromise my bid by seducing me?"

"I know it sounds crazy…"

"*Sounds?* What if I obliged you, and then denied it afterwards? Were you going to the media to expose me? Think of the headlines!"

"I was never very happy about it," she said meekly. "But Sami was so desperate."

"But why not speak to me directly? She could have phoned me!"

"Because she was convinced you had reasons of your own for wanting the marriage. She wasn't sure how you'd take it, or if you'd tell Walid. As soon as I saw you, I understood her fears. Let's face it, you're a bit intimidating these days, Salah."

She kissed his shoulder to soften the words.

He lay in silence for a moment. "And she was right. I did have reasons, not that I understood that then. I think now that I felt it was a way to bring you back into my life. And it did."

"But only because Sami begged me. I wouldn't have come otherwise. What would have happened if I hadn't?"

"I would have found a way, Desi. I know it now. Something had begun to speak in me, and it would not have been silenced until I saw you again.

"But still, I think, we will be grateful to Sami all the rest of our lives. And I am very glad to know that I was not mistaken. I do know you, my heart."

She said thoughtfully, brushing his cheek with a curl of her hair, "It could be a problem, though, never being able to lie to you."

"You foresee that you will want to tell me lies, *Deezee?* When? Why?"

"Well, for instance…when I'm trying to throw a surprise party for your eightieth birthday," she said. "It's going to be a bit of an anti-climax, isn't it, if you know all about it right from the get-go?"

* * * * *

RICK'S APPOINTMENT with his attorney early Wednesday morning went only moderately better than his meeting with social services the day before. The prognosis wasn't great— but at least his attorney was going to file a motion for DNA testing. Just so Rick could petition to see the child…his sister's baby. The sister he didn't know he had until it was too late.

The rest of what his attorney said had been downhill from there.

Cell phone in hand before he'd even reached his Nitro, Rick punched in the speed dial number he'd programmed the day before.

Maybe foster parent Sue Bookman hadn't received his message. Or had lost his number. Maybe she didn't want to talk to him. At this point he didn't much care what she wanted.

"Hello?" She answered before the first ring was complete. And sounded breathless.

Young and breathless.

"Ms. Bookman?"

"Yes. This is Rick Kraynick, right?"

"Yes, ma'am."

"I recognized your number on caller ID," she said, her voice uneven, as though she was still engaged in whatever physical activity had her so breathless to begin with. "I'm sorry I didn't get back to you. I've been a little…distracted."

The words came in more disjointed spurts. Was she jogging?

"No problem," he said, when, in fact, he'd spent the better part of the night before watching his phone. And fretting. "Did I get you at a bad time?"

"No worse than usual," she said, adding, "Better than some. So, how can I help?"

God, if only this could be so easy. He'd ask. She'd help. And life could go well. At least for one little person in his family.

It would be a first.

"Mr. Kraynick?"

"Yes. Sorry. I was… Are you sure there isn't a better time to call?"

"I'm bouncing a baby, Mr. Kraynick. It's what I do."

"Is it Carrie?" he asked quickly, his pulse racing.

"How do you know Carrie?" She sounded defensive, which wouldn't do him any good.

"I'm her uncle," he explained, "her mother's—Christy's—older brother, and I know you have her."

"I can neither confirm nor deny your allegations, Mr. Kraynick. Please call social services." She rattled off the number.

"Wait!" he said, unable to hide his urgency. "Please," he said more calmly. "Just hear me out."

"How did you find me?"

"A friend of Christy's."

"I'm sorry I can't help you, Mr. Kraynick," she said softly. "This conversation is over."

"I grew up in foster care," he said, as though that gave him some special privilege. Some insider's edge.

"Then you know you shouldn't be calling me at all."

"Yes… But Carrie is my niece," he said. "I need to see her. To know that she's okay."

"You'll have to go through social services to arrange that."

"I'm sure you know it's not as easy as it sounds. I'm a single man with no real ties and I've no intention of petitioning for custody. They aren't real eager to give me the time of day. I never even knew Carrie's mother. For all intents and purposes, our mother didn't raise either one of us. All I have going for me is half a set of genes. My lawyer's on it, but it could be weeks—months—before this is sorted out. Carrie could be adopted by then. Which would be fine, great for her, but then I'd have lost my chance. I don't want to take her. I won't hurt her. I just have to see her."

"I'm sorry, Mr. Kraynick, but…"

* * * * *

*Find out if Rick Kraynick will ever have a chance
to meet his niece.
Look for A DAUGHTER'S TRUST
by Tara Taylor Quinn,
available in September 2009.*

We'll be spotlighting a different series
every month throughout 2009
to celebrate our 60th anniversary.

**Look for Harlequin® Superromance®
in September!**

*Celebrate with
The Diamond Legacy
miniseries!*

Follow the stories of four cousins as they come to terms
with the complications of love and what it means to
be a family. Discover with them the sixty-year-old secret
that rocks not one but two families.

A DAUGHTER'S TRUST by *Tara Taylor Quinn*
September

FOR THE LOVE OF FAMILY by *Kathleen O'Brien*
October

LIKE FATHER, LIKE SON by *Karina Bliss*
November

A MOTHER'S SECRET by *Janice Kay Johnson*
December

Available wherever books are sold.

You're invited to join our Tell Harlequin Reader Panel!

By joining our new reader panel you will:

- Receive Harlequin® books—they are FREE and yours to keep with no obligation to purchase anything!
- Participate in fun online surveys
- Exchange opinions and ideas with women just like you
- Have a say in our new book ideas and help us publish the best in women's fiction

In addition, you will have a chance to win great prizes and receive special gifts!
See Web site for details. Some conditions apply.
Space is limited.

To join, visit us at
www.TellHarlequin.com.

Stay up-to-date on all your romance reading news!

The Harlequin Inside Romance newsletter is a **FREE** quarterly newsletter highlighting our upcoming series releases and promotions!

**Go to
eHarlequin.com/InsideRomance**
or e-mail us at
InsideRomance@Harlequin.com
to sign up to receive
your **FREE** newsletter today!

You can also subscribe by writing to us at: HARLEQUIN BOOKS
Attention: Customer Service Department
P.O. Box 9057, Buffalo, NY 14269-9057

Please allow 4-6 weeks for delivery of the first issue by mail.

IRNBPAQ209

Do you crave dark and sensual paranormal tales?

Get your fix with Silhouette Nocturne!

In print:

Two new titles available every month wherever books are sold.

Online:

Nocturne eBooks available monthly from **www.silhouettenocturne.com.**

Nocturne Bites:

Short sensual paranormal stories available monthly online from **www.nocturnebites.com** and in print with the Nocturne Bites collections available April 2009 and October 2009 wherever books are sold.

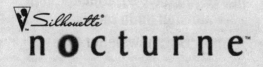

www.silhouettenocturne.com
www.paranormalromanceblog.com

SNBITESRG

REQUEST YOUR FREE BOOKS!

2 FREE NOVELS PLUS 2 FREE GIFTS!

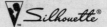

Passionate, Powerful, Provocative!

YES! Please send me 2 FREE Silhouette Desire® novels and my 2 FREE gifts (gifts are worth about $10). After receiving them, if I don't wish to receive any more books, I can return the shipping statement marked "cancel". If I don't cancel, I will receive 6 brand-new novels every month and be billed just $4.05 per book in the U.S. or $4.74 per book in Canada. That's a savings of almost 15% off the cover price! It's quite a bargain! Shipping and handling is just 50¢ per book.* I understand that accepting the 2 free books and gifts places me under no obligation to buy anything. I can always return a shipment and cancel at any time. Even if I never buy another book, the two free books and gifts are mine to keep forever.

225 SDN EYMS   326 SDN EYM4

Name	(PLEASE PRINT)	
Address		Apt. #
City	State/Prov.	Zip/Postal Code

Signature (if under 18, a parent or guardian must sign)

Mail to the Silhouette Reader Service:
IN U.S.A.: P.O. Box 1867, Buffalo, NY 14240-1867
IN CANADA: P.O. Box 609, Fort Erie, Ontario L2A 5X3

Not valid to current subscribers of Silhouette Desire books.

Want to try two free books from another line?
Call 1-800-873-8635 or visit www.morefreebooks.com.

* Terms and prices subject to change without notice. Prices do not include applicable taxes. Sales tax applicable in N.Y. Canadian residents will be charged applicable provincial taxes and GST. Offer not valid in Quebec. This offer is limited to one order per household. All orders subject to approval. Credit or debit balances in a customer's account(s) may be offset by any other outstanding balance owed by or to the customer. Please allow 4 to 6 weeks for delivery. Offer available while quantities last.

Your Privacy: Silhouette Books is committed to protecting your privacy. Our Privacy Policy is available online at www.eHarlequin.com or upon request from the Reader Service. From time to time we make our lists of customers available to reputable third parties who may have a product or service of interest to you. If you would prefer we not share your name and address, please check here. ☐

SDES09R

Silhouette® *Desire*

COMING NEXT MONTH
Available September 8, 2009

#1963 MORE THAN A MILLIONAIRE—Emilie Rose
Man of the Month
The wrong woman is carrying his baby! A medical mix-up wreaks havoc on his plans, and now he'll do anything to gain custody of his heir—even if it means seducing the mother-to-be.

**#1964 TEXAN'S WEDDING-NIGHT WAGER—
Charlene Sands**
Texas Cattleman's Club: Maverick County Millionaires
This Texan won't sign the papers. Before he agrees to a divorce, he wants revenge on his estranged wife. But his plan backfires when she turns the tables on him....

#1965 CONQUERING KING'S HEART—Maureen Child
Kings of California
Passion reignites when long-ago lovers find themselves in each other's arms—and at each other's throats. Don't miss this latest irresistible King hero!

#1966 ONE NIGHT, TWO BABIES—Kathie DeNosky
The Illegitimate Heirs
A steamy one-week affair leaves this heiress alone and pregnant—with twins! When the billionaire father returns,
will a marriage by contract be enough to claim his family?

#1967 IN THE TYCOON'S DEBT—Emily McKay
The once-scorned CEO will give his former bride what she wants...as soon as she gives him the wedding night he's long been denied.

**#1968 THE BILLIONAIRE'S FAKE ENGAGEMENT—
Robyn Grady**
When news breaks of an ex-lover carrying his child, this billionaire proposes to his mysterious mistress to create a distraction. Yet will he still want her to wear his ring when she reveals the secrets of her past?

SDCNMBPA0809